Welcome back to Penhally Bay!

Mills & Boon® Medical™ Romance welcomes you
back to the picturesque town of Penhally, nestled
on the rugged Cornish coast! With sandy beaches
and breathtaking landscapes Penhally is a warm,
bustling community, cared for by the Penhally
Bay Surgery team, led by the distinguished and
commanding Dr Nick Tremayne.

We're bringing you four new books
set in this idyllic coastal town, where fishing boats
bob up and down in the bay, friendly faces line the
cobbled streets and romance flutters on the
Cornish sea breeze! We've got gorgeous
Mediterranean heroes, top-notch city surgeons, and
the return of Penhally's very own bad-boy rebel!
But that's not all…

We step back into the life of enigmatic,
guarded hero Dr Nick Tremayne, and nurse
Kate Althorpe—the one woman who has stolen
Nick's heart and the only woman he won't
allow himself to love! Dr Nick's unquestionable
professional skill and dedication to the
Penhally Bay Surgery hide his private pain—
his is a story that will pierce your heart.

So turn the page and meet them for yourself…

**And if you've never visited Penhally before,
step right in and enjoy Medical™ Romance's
most popular mini-series. There is a world of
romantic treats awaiting you.**

Dear Reader

When my editor asked me if I'd like to be part of the second series of *Penhally*, I was thrilled—I loved the area and all the characters, so it was a joy to revisit them.

As I was writing this book, *Strictly Come Dancing* was on TV; my daughter and I loved the music and the dresses and the dancing. It struck me that Charlotte and James needed something frothy to balance their fairly dark conflicts, and a dancing competition gave me a great reason to get James into Charlotte's life and help her lower her barriers, bit by bit. (And it was fun making my husband help me choreograph the dancing!)

It was also great to revisit Dragan and Melinda from the last series—and fellow author Margaret McDonagh and I were adamant that we wanted Bramble to have puppies. As I live in an all-dog household, I borrowed the cat from my friend Biddy and her back story from my friend Jan.

I loved the fact that this book was set on a cardiac ward. My late mother was the senior sister in our local cardiac ward, so it felt like a nod to her—especially given the fact that Kate's health in the book reflected my mum's.

You'll need tissues. I cried my eyes out in places. But this book is also about the power of love, and how it makes everything better.

I'm always delighted to hear from readers, so do come and visit me at www.katehardy.com

With love

Kate Hardy

FALLING FOR THE PLAYBOY MILLIONAIRE

BY
KATE HARDY

In loving memory of Sandra Christine Sewell, 1945–1986.
The best of mothers, still so very much missed.
And with thanks to Caroline Anderson, Margaret McDonagh and
Anne Fraser for making the second series of Penhally such fun!

First published in Great Britain 2009
Harlequin Mills & Boon Limited,
Eton House, 18-24 Paradise Road, Richmond, Surrey TW9 1SR

© Kate Hardy 2009

ISBN: 978 0 263 20947 1

Set in Times Roman
15-1009-53714

Harlequin Mills & B
renewable and recyc
sustainable forests. T
to the legal environn

Printed and bound i
by CPI Antony Rov

Kate Hardy lives in Norwich, in the east of England, with her husband, two young children, one bouncy spaniel, and too many books to count! When she's not busy writing romance or researching local history, she helps out at her children's schools. She also loves cooking—spot the recipes sneaked into her books! (They're also on her website, along with extracts and stories behind the books.) Writing for Mills & Boon has been a dream come true for Kate—something she wanted to do ever since she was twelve. She's been writing Medical™ Romances for nearly five years now, and also writes for Modern Heat™. She says it's the best of both worlds, because she gets to learn lots of new things when she's researching the background to a book: add a touch of passion, drama and danger, a new gorgeous hero every time, and it's the perfect job!

Kate's always delighted to hear from readers, so do drop in to her website at www.katehardy.com

Recent titles by the same author:

Medical™ Romance
THE CHILDREN'S DOCTOR'S SPECIAL PROPOSAL
  (*The London Victoria* duet)
THE GREEK DOCTOR'S NEW-YEAR BABY
  (*The London Victoria* duet)
THE SPANISH DOCTOR'S LOVE-CHILD
THE DOCTOR'S ROYAL LOVE-CHILD
  (*Brides of Penhally Bay*)

Modern Heat™
TEMPORARY BOSS, PERMANENT MISTRESS
PLAYBOY BOSS, PREGNANCY OF PASSION
  (*To Tame a Playboy* duet)
SURRENDER TO THE PLAYBOY SHEIKH
  (*To Tame a Playboy* duet)

BRIDES OF PENHALLY BAY

*Bachelor doctors become husbands and fathers—
in a place where hearts are made whole.*

**Another four books set in the picturesque town of
Penhally, nestled on the rugged Cornish coast.**

**Recently we've been back in Penhally as bad-boy doc
Sam Cavendish tried to win back his long-lost wife…**
The Rebel of Penhally Bay by Caroline Anderson

**Then midwife Annie met
gorgeous Spanish doctor Dr Raphael Castillo,
and one magical night led to one little miracle…**
Spanish Doctor, Pregnant Midwife by Anne Fraser

**This month there's a real treat in store as
gorgeous high-flying heart surgeon James
arrives in Penhally!**
Falling for the Playboy Millionaire by Kate Hardy

**And next month there's a new GP in town
when Italian doctor and single father Luca d'Azzaro
brings his twin babies to Penhally**
A Mother for the Italian's Twins by Margaret McDonagh

From Mills & Boon® Medical™ Romance

CHAPTER ONE

'Isn't that Sophia over there?' The blonde indicated the far side of the room with her champagne glass.

James knew he ought to change the subject or just walk away, but he couldn't help himself. He looked.

And there she was. Sophia Alexander, society's favourite party girl. Draped over yet another good-looking man, laughing as if she didn't have a care in the world.

Which, to be fair, she probably didn't.

'Mmm,' James replied, trying to sound noncommittal.

'She's not with that Italian model any more, then.'

The one she'd been photographed with on his father's yacht, a mere six months after their wedding. The pictures of his topless wife and her lover had been splashed across newspapers around the globe.

Though that was old news. Very old news. After the Italian, Sophia had had an affair with a Spanish actor: lover number two on his divorce papers. And then a Brazilian footballer, who'd been squiring her around in the week before what should've been her first wedding anniversary with James.

'I hear he's a French chef,' the blonde added.

Indeed. No doubt the guy would be cooking Sophia a 'happy divorce' meal tonight. Among other things.

Ha. And to think James had come out tonight to celebrate his freedom—the sheer relief that his marriage was legally over. He should've guessed that his ex-wife would be partying even harder. Showing him in the best way she knew that she didn't give a damn, and she was going to enjoy every penny of her extremely generous settlement.

'What do you think it'll be next? A Greek restaurateur?' the blonde asked.

If this was the woman's way of trying to find out if he really was over his ex-wife, she could've found a more tactful way to ask. James was about to say something extremely cutting—and then he saw something in the woman's eyes. Something that told him she wasn't merely a guest, or just supremely tactless. The blonde was a journalist, after a story, and she knew very well what today was for him.

Decree absolute day.

The day he'd hoped that Sophia would change her surname back to Carvell-Jones, and the press would stop tormenting him.

How naive he'd been.

'I really have no idea. I don't keep tabs on my ex-wife,' James drawled, with emphasis on the *ex*. 'Excuse me. There's someone I need to see by the bar.'

It was a lie, and they both knew it. But she let him go without further question, and he made his escape from the party as soon as he could.

No doubt the tabloids would all be full of the story to-morrow. How poor, heartbroken surgeon James Alexander had been forced to watch his ex-wife celebrating with yet another of her lovers on the day their divorce was finalised. And then there would be speculation about who would mend the heart surgeon's heart.

You couldn't get much further from the truth. James was hardly poor, despite the settlement, and he was very far from heartbroken. He'd stopped caring about Sophia a long time ago. It was just a pity that he'd been too smitten with her to see her for what she was before he'd married her: a spoiled social-ite who didn't think any further ahead than the next party.

'What was I supposed to do, James? You never paid me any attention. You practically pushed me into his arms.' The words echoed in his head: words she'd flung at him when he'd confronted her about the yacht episode and demanded to know what the hell she was playing at.

But she'd married a surgeon, not a socialite. James had never made a secret of the fact that his career was important to him. Cardiothoracic surgery was the most competitive specialty going, and he'd excelled at it—taking all his exams early and coming top in every single one. He loved what he did. He loved making a difference, giving someone their future back. Surely Sophia had been able to understand that he couldn't leave a patient halfway through an operation just because she didn't want to be late for a party? For pity's sake, he wouldn't leave the hospital until his patient was out of the recovery room and had been settled for at least an hour. He was a *surgeon*, and he believed in living up to the responsibilities that went with it.

Or maybe she'd thought that he would change, for her. That he'd switch specialties, go into plastics or something similar, and have a high-profile clinic on Harley Street. A job where he'd work nine to five at most, where all his surgical cases were elective rather than emergency, where he'd earn obscene amounts of money from pandering to the vanity of celebrities.

Just as he'd been naive enough to think that Sophia would understand the demands of his job as a children's heart surgeon and make allowances for them, instead of flouncing off in pique, straight into the arms of the first gorgeous hunk who smiled at her.

Their marriage had crashed as spectacularly and publicly as it had begun. And the only reason James hadn't served Sophia with divorce papers the week she'd been cavorting with her Italian and the paparazzi had taken snap after snap after snap had been because the law said you couldn't get a divorce until you'd been married for a year. He'd had to wait for six excruciating months before he could apply for a divorce. Six months where he'd been forced to endure his wife flaunting a string of lovers in the gossip magazines.

At least Sophia hadn't contested his grounds. Then again, with the amount of evidence in the press, she could hardly have denied adultery.

James let the front door click to behind him and deadlocked it. Right at that moment, he was sick of London. Sick of parties. Sick of everything—even the glittery charity fundraisers he'd once loved doing for his hospital. He could really do with some time away. Sure, he could call his father and go to one of the family's private resorts, but he knew he'd still have to face the same old thing. Parties like tonight's, full of debs and celebs.

What he really wanted was to chill out, somewhere quiet and peaceful. Somewhere where there weren't any supermodels or society party girls who did nothing but shop and look for rich husbands they were going to cheat on within months of their flamboyant and expensive weddings.

Not that such a place existed.

Or did it?

He'd trained with Jack Tremayne in London. Jack had known how to party with the best of them; but then he'd moved back to Cornwall, to where he'd grown up. James hadn't gone to Jack's wedding in Penhally, simply because he hadn't been able to face the happy couple while his own marriage had been collapsing around his ears. He'd sent an expensive present and a feeble excuse.

Though he'd also wondered why on earth Jack had been mad enough to bury himself in such a backwater. Why go back to a little seaside town when he could've had so many more opportunities in London?

But maybe Jack had the right idea.

Maybe in Cornwall, miles away from London, James could find some peace.

He picked up the phone and dialled Jack's number. It rang

and rang, and he was just about to give up when a sleepy voice answered. 'Hello?'

James glanced at his watch. For pity's sake, it was a Saturday night and it wasn't even midnight. The Jack Tremayne he knew would barely have started partying at this time of the evening. 'Jack? It's James. Sorry, did I wake you?'

'Don't worry. Just napping when Helena sleeps,' Jack mumbled.

Of course. The new baby. It had slipped his mind. 'Sorry, mate,' he said, guilt flooding through him.

'Everything all right?' Jack asked.

'Yes.' *No.* 'Look, I was wondering… You said a few months back, if I wanted to come and spend a few days…'

'Uh…'

'Sorry, I shouldn't have asked,' James said immediately. How selfish and thoughtless could he get? 'Not when you have a new baby.'

'No, no, of course you can come and stay. Alison won't mind.'

James rather thought she might. And he didn't blame her. 'Look, don't worry, I'll stay in a hotel or something. But it'd be nice to catch up. Have a beer together.'

'Yeah, sure.' Jack seemed to be waking up now. 'Are you all right, James? You sound a bit flat.'

'Just had enough of London.' He wasn't going to mention the divorce. It wasn't fair to dump that on a sleep-deprived new father. Even though Jack was about the only person he knew who'd understand what it was like to have the press on your back—Jack had had his fair share of flak from the tabloids in the past. 'Hey, I'll let you get back to sleep. I'll call you at a more sociable hour tomorrow.'

Jack laughed. 'You mean when you crawl out of bed in the middle of the afternoon.'

James forced himself to laugh back. 'Something like that.'

'If you're serious about wanting to get out of London, I

might be able to help. There was a job on the bulletin board at work last week that's right up your street. Registrar on the cardiac surgery team. Why don't you come down and take a look?'

It would be a sideways move. But the chances were, in a smaller place, he'd get more responsibility. At twenty-nine, James knew he needed more experience before he took the next step up, and this could be a really good opportunity. 'I might just do that.'

'St Piran's is a good place to work,' Jack said. 'I'm really happy here.'

Yeah. Because Jack had met the love of his life.

As if Jack had picked up on James's thoughts, he continued, 'And you never know, you might find someone here who'll be able to make you forget Sophia.'

James gave a mirthless laugh. 'You must be joking. I'm not getting involved with anyone, ever again. Been there, done that.' And the whole lot had been documented in the press. In every single squalid, sordid detail. He didn't believe in love any more. 'No, from now on, it's no strings and no involvement.'

To his relief, Jack didn't argue. 'Give me a ring tomorrow, when I've had a chance to talk to Alison.'

'Yeah, sure.'

'And think about the job. It might be just what you need.'

Maybe, James thought as he replaced the receiver, just maybe, his friend had a point.

'Did you hear a single word I just said?' Nick asked his niece, looking pained.

'I…No,' Charlotte admitted. 'Sorry, Nick. I didn't mean to be rude.'

'Just that your head's full of plans for the new centre.'

Yes, she thought. And the new cardiac surgeon at St Piran's, James Alexander. Why on earth the head of surgery had given the job to a man who spent more time at parties than with his patients, she'd never know. The son of a supermodel and an international businessman, James was prime fodder for the gossip pages—and she'd seen his face splashed across enough magazines brought in by visitors to the ward. Usually posed on a red carpet, in full evening dress with a smile so perfect that it had to be the result of expensive cosmetic dental work, and some gorgeous supermodel with legs up to her armpits draped over his arm.

A man like that, used to partying with A-listers in exclusive clubs and hotels, would be bored stiff around here within a matter of hours. He wouldn't see the beauty of this quiet corner of Cornwall—just that it was a backwater.

And then he'd be off again in search of the bright lights, dropping his responsibilities without a second thought and leaving everyone else to pick up the pieces. Marvellous.

'Charlotte?'

'Sorry.' She gave her uncle a rueful smile. 'I'm wool-gathering again.'

'It's not just the centre, is it?'

For a moment, she thought about fibbing. But Nick Tremayne had been good to her. He'd offered her a bolthole when she'd needed it most, two years ago, when she'd left Liverpool after the court case. And, considering that right now she was sitting in her uncle's kitchen and drinking his coffee, the least she could do was be honest. 'I'm fretting because of the new guy at work,' she admitted.

'You're worried about him?' He reached over and squeezed her hand.

She smiled at her uncle, knowing exactly what he'd been too tactful to say aloud. 'Not in *that* way, Nick.' She was well past the days when she'd been too nervous to stay in a room with anyone male. 'No, I just think he's going to be a waste of space. A party boy. I wish they'd chosen someone who would at least be dedicated to the job and work with the team, instead of grabbing all the glory for his personal headlines.'

Nick raised an eyebrow. 'I'm the last person to make a comment there, considering how I behaved towards Jack.'

'He's forgiven you. And you're close now. That's all that matters.'

'Maybe,' Nick suggested, 'this guy won't be quite as bad as you think.'

She scoffed. 'Even allowing for press exaggeration, I don't think James Alexander's going to fit in.' Catching her uncle's expression, she frowned. 'What?'

'Did you say James Alexander?' Nick queried.

'Yes. Do you know him?'

'He's a friend of Jack's. Or, at least, he was, in London.'

'Back in Jack's wild days?' At Nick's nod, she said, 'Then I rest my case.'

'People change, Charlotte. Give the man a chance.'

'Hmm.' She switched the subject, not wanting to be drawn. In her experience, men didn't usually change. Well, Nick had, a bit—he'd learned to get along with his children and pull together as a family after his wife's death, but it had taken a lot of effort on the part of Jack, Lucy and Edward. Jack had settled down, too, thanks to Alison, but in Charlotte's view Nick and Jack were the exceptions that proved the rule. 'It's two weeks until the rape crisis centre opens. My friend Maggie's almost finished setting up the website.'

'That's good.' Nick smiled at her. 'Annabel would've been so proud of you, you know. She always said you were sensible and clever and kind.'

'So was she.' Charlotte had adored her aunt. She still missed Annabel's kindness and her common sense.

'You remind me of her,' Nick said softly. 'Not just because of the way you look. You've got the same inner strength she had. And I'm as proud of you as she would've been. It takes a lot of guts to do something like this when…' His voice faded.

'When I've been through it myself?' Charlotte wrapped her arms round herself. 'That's why I'm doing it, Nick. Because

I've been there. Yes, it hurts. It brings back things I'd rather not remember. But because of…' Her mouth filled with bile and she swallowed it back. 'Look, it's just easier talking to someone who's been there and doesn't make you spell every single thing out. If I shrink away from this, I'm letting Michael win.' She lifted her chin. 'And that's not going to happen, Nick. I'm not letting him win. I'm going to help other people get over it, just as people helped me get over what happened to me.'

'But you're still not completely over it, are you?' Nick asked. 'You haven't dated since it happened. Three years is a long time, love.'

'And your way's better, is it?' Charlotte parried. 'Dating as many people as possible, so you don't have time to think?'

Colour shot into his face. 'There's no need to be rude.'

She winced at the rebuke. 'Sorry. I shouldn't have said that. Not to you, of all people. Without you, I wouldn't have a place for the centre.' Nick, as the senior partner at the surgery in Penhally, had generously agreed to let her use a room in the surgery every Wednesday for the rape crisis centre. And in return she'd promised to run some sessions in the surgery at Penhally about heart health, including some especially for post-menopausal women at Gemma's well-woman clinic.

'You would've found somewhere you could use.'

'But Penhally's perfect. There's something about the place—something… It's going to sound daft, but something *healing*.'

He smiled wryly. 'You're not daft. And I suppose you have a point—I do date a lot. Too much, maybe. But I've never forgotten your aunt.' He sighed deeply. 'She's going to haunt me for the rest of my life.'

She reached over to squeeze his hand. 'Nick, Annabel wouldn't have wanted you to be miserable. What happened to her was terrible, but it wasn't anyone's fault. It was just one of those stupid, senseless things that make the world a darker place. But she wouldn't have wanted you to be like this—and, yes, before you start arguing, I *can* say that because I knew her.

She thinks—thought,' she corrected herself swiftly, 'in the same way my mum does. She would've wanted you to find someone who'd love you as much as she did. You have to learn to let go of the past and move on.' She smiled wryly. 'Listen to me—talk about pots and kettles.' She hadn't exactly moved on after Michael, had she? 'But doctors aren't very good at taking their own advice, are they?'

'No,' Nick admitted. 'We aren't.'

'Maybe,' Charlotte said, 'we both need to make more of an effort.'

'Maybe.' He lifted his mug of coffee. 'Here's to you, the new centre—and a decent working relationship with James Alexander.'

'And here's to you, the new centre, and finding someone who can make you as happy as Annabel did,' Charlotte responded, lifting her own mug.

CHAPTER TWO

'AREN'T you supposed to be at lunch?' Steffie, the senior sister on the cardiothoracic ward, leaned against the door of Charlotte's office with her arms folded, tapping her foot.

Charlotte looked up from her notes and flapped a hand at the packet of sandwiches in front of her. 'Look. Food. I *am* at lunch.'

'You're working,' Steffie corrected. 'You're not taking a proper break.'

'It's temporary. Just until the centre's up and running properly. This next couple of weeks I've got a ton of loose ends to tie up, and it's easiest to sort things out in my lunch break rather than the evenings, in case I need to get hold of someone during office hours.'

'Hmm. As long as it *is* temporary. I worry about you,' Steffie said.

'Hey, no need to worry about me. I'm absolutely fine.' Charlotte gave her friend a broad smile. 'And you know me. I like being busy.'

'Hmm.' Steffie didn't sound convinced. 'Well, you're going to be even busier tomorrow.'

'Tomorrow?'

Steffie rolled her eyes. 'Don't tell me you've forgotten that he's starting? James Alexander. The new heart surgeon.'

Charlotte shrugged. 'I expect he'll be round to see us at some point, then.'

'I know you missed him when he came round after his interview, but you must have seen his picture in the papers, Charlotte. He's the most gorgeous man ever to have set foot in this hospital. How on earth can you stay so cool about him when every other female in the place is getting palpitations?'

'Easy,' Charlotte said dryly. 'I go for dark chocolate and a good book instead of a mug of coffee and the gossip rags.'

Steffie laughed. 'You're impossible. But I bet our Mr Alexander will melt even you.'

'This is where I should bet you a small fortune and clean up,' Charlotte retorted with a smile, 'except it'd be too unfair— like taking sweeties from a toddler. He's not going to melt me, because he's not my type.'

'So what *is* your type, Charlotte?' Steffie asked.

Nobody. Because she didn't date. Charlotte couldn't resist teasing her friend. 'I'll let you into a secret,' she said, beckoning.

Steffie came over to Charlotte's desk and stooped, ready to listen.

'I can't date because I'm already married,' Charlotte whispered.

Steffie's eyes grew wider. 'You're *kidding!*'

'Cross my heart. I'm absolutely serious,' Charlotte said.

'But—you've been working here for nearly two years and you've never talked about your husband. None of us have even met him.'

'Oh, but you have.' Charlotte smiled broadly. 'You see, Steffie, I'm married to my job.'

Steffie groaned and cuffed her playfully. 'Like I said. You're impossible!'

'No. I'm just more interested in my job than in a man with an ego the size of Mars.'

Steffie blinked. 'Have you actually met him, then? Or heard something on the grapevine from someone you trained with?'

'Neither. But it stands to reason. James Alexander is rich, spoiled, and spends his entire life squiring celebs to exclusive parties.' Charlotte ticked them off on her fingers. 'Of course his ego's going to be the size of Mars.'

'Four thousand, two hundred and twenty miles in diameter. A little over half the diameter of Earth but, I grant you, still pretty big in terms of ego,' a voice drawled from the doorway.

'Oh, lord!' Steffie said, colour flooding her face as she looked at the man standing in the doorway, who'd obviously overheard quite a bit of their conversation.

'Hello. I'm James Alexander,' he said—as if either of them needed telling.

'Stephanie Jones, senior sister on the cardiac ward—everyone calls me Steffie.' Steffie shook his proffered hand. 'Um, nice to meet you.'

'And you.' James smiled warmly at her, then turned to Charlotte and raised an eyebrow, as if enquiring who she was.

For a moment, her tongue was glued to the roof of her mouth.

Steffie was right about one thing. James Alexander *was* the most gorgeous man ever to have set foot in St Piran's. Tall, with dark hair and deep brown eyes, he could've walked straight out of the pages of an upmarket magazine. His clothes were expensively cut, his shoes were highly polished and she'd just bet they were handmade, and as for his hair…

James Alexander was definitely a man who believed in being groomed. There wasn't a single hair out of place. He was perfectly clean-shaven. And Charlotte was horrified to find the pads of her fingers tingling, as if tempting her to trail them over his face and discover for herself just how soft his skin was.

Worse still, James was looking at her with a quizzical air. Waiting for her to introduce herself. Oh, great. He'd caught her ogling him. And considering that she never, ever ogled men…She could do with the earth opening up and swallowing her—preferably five minutes ago.

'Charlotte Walker, cardiology registrar,' she said, rather more brusquely than she'd intended, and winced inwardly at the sound of her voice.

What was it about this man that had her making such a fool of herself?

She knew better than this.

Keep it cool, calm and professional, she reminded herself silently.

And then had to remind herself of that again when he shook her hand and her pulse rate speeded up a notch.

She had to be sickening for something. No way did she react this way towards men she didn't know—or even to men she *did* know. She kept things tidy and professional, with a smile on her face and plenty of distance. Her knees didn't normally go weak when a good-looking man smiled at her. So what was going on here? 'I believe we were expecting you at some point tomorrow,' she said, to cover her confusion.

He shrugged. 'I was in the area. I thought I'd drop in and introduce myself—then I can hit the ground running instead of wasting a day in introductions.'

Now, that she hadn't expected. And it made her feel just the tiniest bit guilty about what she'd said. Maybe she *had* been unfair to him. She had no idea how much he'd overheard of her conversation with Steffie, but she knew what she needed to do. The decent thing.

'I'm sorry about what I said. I shouldn't have made assumptions about you.'

'I'm used to it. It still amazes me how people believe every single word they read in the press, but…' he shrugged '…I guess not everyone likes to form their own opinion.'

Ouch. Though she knew she deserved the rebuke. 'I'm impressed that you actually knew the size of Mars.'

He spread his hands. 'Hang around with stars, you get to learn a bit about planets, too.'

'Touché.' Steffie laughed. 'Charlotte, I do believe you've met your match. Charlotte's our resident brainbox,' she explained for James's benefit. 'She's the captain of our inter-departmental quiz team, and we haven't lost once since Charlotte's been on the team.'

'That sounds like a challenge,' James said, his brown eyes lighting up.

'Absolutely not,' Charlotte cut in crisply, hating the idea of anyone seeing her as a challenge. Been there, done that, never going to repeat it. 'The whole point of the quiz night is to raise money for charity. It's not about showing off.'

'With my ego the size of Mars, that is.'

Clearly that had hit home and he wasn't going to let her forget it any time soon. She lifted a shoulder. 'Think yourself lucky I only said Mars, not Jupiter.'

'Ouch.' He smiled at her. 'Buy me a coffee, Charlotte, and I'll forgive you.'

Was he coming on to her?

Her shock must have shown on her face because he explained, 'It's lunchtime and, as I'm the new boy and I'm going to be working pretty closely with your department, I'd really appreciate someone showing me around.'

'What about Theatre?' Surely someone in the surgical department should be the one to show the new surgeon around?

'I've already been there,' James said. 'Actually, I was a bit naughty and got an old friend to show me around. Jack Tremayne. He introduced me to the anaesthetists and the theatre staff. And he said that I should come and find you, as you'd show me around here and take me to the intensive care unit and the children's ward.'

'Did he, now?' Her cousin had better not be matchmaking. Jack might be deliriously happy with his new wife and a ready-made family and their newborn daughter, but it didn't mean that everyone wanted to get married and have babies. Charlotte certainly didn't want to get married. Ever.

James spread his hands. 'Hey. Don't shoot the messenger. If you have a problem with your cousin…'

'No. But I was—'

'In the middle of your own lunch break,' Steffie cut in. 'And working through that, too. So this is a double-win situation— it means you're not working too hard, and James gets to see the hospital properly. Show the poor man around, Charlotte.'

It took an effort to get herself back into professional mode, but Charlotte managed it. 'I assume you've already met the consultants?'

'At my interview, yes.'

'Good.' She took him on a whistle-stop tour of the cardiothoracic ward, the intensive care unit and finally the children's ward, introducing him to all the staff. He was as polite and smiley as she was, she noticed; clearly this was his professional face. One she could definitely work with. She liked the way she treated the nurses and auxiliary staff as his equals, rather than looking down on them. Acknowledging that he might be the surgeon who'd do the operation, but they were the staff who would look after the patient outside Theatre and would spot problems before they grew into emergencies.

As for this odd feeling every time she had when she looked into his eyes—well, that would go when she got used to him. It was just because he was a new face at the hospital, she told herself. The fact that she hadn't reacted this way to any other member of staff was beside the point.

'Right. Café. How do you take your coffee?'

'I was joking,' James said hastily. 'I've stolen your lunch break, so *I'll* buy the coffees.'

'No, it's fine.' She gave him her best professional smile. 'The deal was showing you around the hospital and buying you coffee.'

'Then thank you. I accept, with pleasure. Black, no sugar, please.' He paused as they queued up. 'Shall I find us a table?'

'Sure. Did you want anything to eat?'

'No, I'm fine, thanks.'

But when Charlotte joined him at the table, James realised with surprise that she was only carrying one cup of coffee, not two.

'Sorry, I really do have to get back to the ward,' she said, with a pointed glance at her watch. 'I have a clinic starting in ten minutes, and there are some notes I need to check first.'

'Sure,' James said. 'I understand.' Even though he had the distinct feeling that she was using her job as an excuse not to stay and have a coffee with him. Because she was embarrassed about her assumptions maybe? But he was used to people thinking he was a playboy until they got to know him and realised that he was absolutely serious about his job, and it didn't bother him any more. He hoped he'd made it clear that he wasn't going to hold it against her. 'Thanks for showing me around—and for the coffee.'

'Pleasure.' She gave him another smile. A professional one—that didn't quite reach her eyes, unlike the one she'd given her colleagues on their tour.

Was Charlotte Walker nervous with people she didn't know, he wondered, or was it just with him?

'Well, enjoy your first day tomorrow,' she said.

'Thanks. And no doubt I'll see you at some point.'

'If any of my patients are on your list.' She gave a half-shrug. 'See you.'

James watched her walk out of the canteen without a backward glance. Well, she'd made it very clear she saw him only as a colleague. And, although she'd been utterly professional in the way she'd shown him round, introducing him to every single one of the staff, she'd been reserved with him.

What made her so wary of him? Was she really narrow-minded enough to believe the rubbish she'd read in the press? And yet the way her colleagues had greeted her... They obviously respected her. Which they wouldn't do if she was narrow-minded or difficult to work with.

Charlotte Walker was a definite puzzle.

And, he acknowledged wryly, she was also gorgeous. Just his type. Slender, with honey-blonde hair worn in a profes-sional-looking French pleat—hair that he'd just bet was soft and silky. He'd itched to release it from its confines and let it trickle through his hands. And she had a perfect rosebud mouth. Even white teeth. Eyes the colour of the midsummer sky.

She was absolutely stunning.

And remote.

And he really should know better. He was at St Piran's to work, not to get involved with someone. Hadn't he promised himself he'd never make the mistake of trusting a woman again?

'Keep it professional,' he advised himself, and drained his coffee before leaving the canteen and walking in the opposite direction from the one Charlotte had taken.

CHAPTER THREE

TUESDAY morning saw Charlotte in early, preparing to see one of her patients who was having open heart surgery that morning. Three-year-old Daisy Freeman and her parents had met most of the surgical team the previous day—Fran Somers, the anaesthetist, and Carlo Orsini, the perfusionist—and today they would meet the man who was going to repair the hole in Daisy's heart with a graft.

James Alexander.

Given that today was his first day, he really was going to have to hit the ground running. He'd be practically straight into Theatre, and he'd have just about enough time to introduce himself to the Freemans before he had to start his list.

Charlotte logged into the computer and opened the file, but she wasn't really seeing the images on the screen. Instead, her head was filled with pictures of James. He'd looked utterly sincere when he'd talked to her on Friday, but he still unsettled her. Not because she thought he was the sort who'd hurt her the way Michael had, but because of her own reaction to him. That weird pull she'd felt towards him... It was crazy. Ridiculous. Even though James had made it clear that the press exaggerated its reports on his lifestyle, she knew there was some truth behind the tales. James Alexander was a playboy, and he'd been part of the fast set Jack had been involved with in London.

Into flash cars and fashionable clothes, and always partying in the hottest places.

Definitely not a man to trust with your heart.

Ha. Not that she'd ever trust a man with her heart again. Not after Michael.

She was happily single, and she intended to stay that way.

Even as she was thinking it, the back of her neck prickled. She looked up, and saw James leaning against the doorpost, his hand poised to knock.

'Good morning, Charlotte,' he said.

She moistened her suddenly dry lips. 'Good morning, James.'

'I've just checked my list for this morning. My notes say that you're Daisy Freeman's cardiologist.'

'Yes.'

'Good.' He smiled at her. 'You're in early—were you planning to go and see her this morning?'

'Yes. I saw her last night, with her parents, and we talked about what's happening today.' She'd ended up staying beyond the end of her shift, but it didn't matter—it was more important to her to reassure them and help Daisy settle in, the night before her op. 'But it's a big day for them and I want to go and hold their hand while she goes into Theatre.'

'I'll come with you. I'm sure you've already prepared them for the op, but in my experience the parents never sleep the night before, they worry themselves sick, and there are always some last-minute questions. Which,' he said, 'is where I come in. Besides, I prefer to meet my patients and their parents before premed, so I can reassure them. I've read the file so I know the clinical details of Daisy's case. We've been waiting to see if the ASD will close on its own, yes?'

In four out of five babies with Daisy's condition, a small atrial septal defect or 'hole in the heart' would close itself by the time the child was eighteen months old; but if the hole was still there when the child was three, it would need surgery.

'Sadly, it hasn't. I did consider trying catheterisation with a septal occluder,' Charlotte said, 'but the last echo showed me that the hole's too big for it to work.'

'I reviewed the images yesterday,' James said, 'and I agree.'

Two surprises: firstly, that a playboy like James would look at a patient's notes when he wasn't even on duty; and, secondly, that he'd agree with her judgement instead of throwing his weight around to make a point—especially as he had a reputation as a hotshot surgeon. Maybe she really had misjudged him.

'I note as well that Daisy's had a lot of chest infections, so I want to double-check her obs this morning to make absolutely sure she's fit for surgery.'

So his attention to detail wasn't just to his grooming. Good. 'When I saw her last night, she was fine—there wasn't even the hint of a sniffle.'

'Fingers crossed she hasn't developed one overnight. Is there anything else I need to know about Daisy or her family— any particular worries I can help with?'

Charlotte really hadn't expected him to be so considerate of his patient and her parents. She'd thought that James would be more interested in the technical side of things and showing off his surgical skills. The fact he wasn't... That was a real bonus. This was a man she could definitely work with.

The fact he was gorgeous to look at too... Well, that was beside the point.

She forced her thoughts back to work. 'Just the usual parental worries about how successful the surgery's going to be, how quickly Daisy will recover, and how much difference it'll really make to her.'

'I'll keep that in mind.' He looked serious. 'What about Daisy herself—does she have one of those rag dolls with the scars? They're really good for helping little ones prepare for an op.'

Another unexpected twist: not only did James know about

the dolls, he clearly encouraged them. 'Yes—her parents have been preparing her for the op for the last week, when we did an ECG and echo and I really wasn't happy with the results.'

James nodded. 'That's about the right length of time to prepare a three-year-old. Role play's one of the best ways of helping them come to terms with an operation and the fact they're going to have scars.'

'She's got a doll with blonde hair and blue eyes, just like her—and she asked me a few questions when I played with her yesterday,' Charlotte volunteered.

James smiled. 'Great. So does her doll have a name?'

'Poppy.'

The fact he'd asked such a simple question showed her that James really was taking his job seriously. He really cared how his patients felt. And Charlotte found herself warming to him.

'And she knows she's going to be in Intensive Care for a couple of days after the op?' he checked.

'Yes. Hannah from the children's ITU took them on a tour yesterday, so Daisy and her parents know exactly what to expect and they won't be worried by all the monitors and tubes.'

'Good. So shall we go and see her?'

'Sure.' It was only then that Charlotte noticed: James was wearing an expensively cut dark suit and what she suspected was a handmade white shirt, but his tie wasn't the sober silk affair she'd expected. It was silk, yes, but it was bright red and covered with bold yellow teddy bears.

'What?' James asked.

'Just…' She paused and raised an eyebrow. 'Admiring your tie.'

'Oh, that.' He shrugged. 'Daisy's three years old and, even though she's probably used to hospitals with her medical history, coming in for an op is still pretty scary. So the teddies are going to make her smile and feel a bit safer with me.'

He'd thought that much about a small detail?

'And before you ask—no, I wouldn't be wearing this to see

a teenage boy. I'd switch to a plain tie, flash my James Bond watch around, and talk to him about Aston Martins.'

Now, that she could believe. James probably owned a different sports car for each day of the week. Like Fleming's super-spy, James Alexander had a string of gorgeous girl-friends. And even though he'd gone into a caring profession, he'd chosen one of the most high-profile specialties. The glitz and glamour stuff rather than being someone who quietly made a difference behind the scenes.

'We'd better get going,' she said. She logged out of the computer and stood up; James stood aside courteously and let her lead the way to the children's ward.

Daisy's bed was in a bay at the far end of the ward, and with every step they took Charlotte was aware of the admiring glances cast in James's direction. Unsurprising, because he looked like a fashion plate, and the tie added a hint of quirki-ness that would melt practically every female heart on the ward.

'Charlotte, can I have a quick word?' Lisa, one of the new foundation stage two doctors, asked.

'Sure, Lisa. Excuse me, James.' She stepped to one side with the younger doctor. 'What can I do for you?'

'Is *he* the new heart surgeon?'

Oh, wonderful. She'd been expecting a quick discussion about a patient, not about James! 'Yes. We're here to see Daisy before her op.'

Lisa sighed. 'He's *gorgeous.* You lucky thing, having to work with him—I definitely wouldn't mind getting up for breakfast if I was sharing it with him!'

What? Surely Lisa didn't think there was something going on between them. 'I didn't share breakfast with him.' Though, now Lisa had put the idea into her head, she could imagine it. James making coffee in her kitchen, wearing nothing but a pair of jeans and a sexy smile, a slight hint of stubble on his cheeks and his hair unruly. James, stealing a bite from her toast, tempting her to lick the crumbs from the corner of his mouth before taking her in his arms and kissing her stupid...

Oh, help. Since when did she fantasise like that? 'It's strictly work,' Charlotte said firmly, as much to keep herself in check as to put Lisa in the picture.

'Looking like that, he was probably snapped up at the age of twelve,' Lisa said ruefully. 'Whenever I've seen him in *Great!* magazine, he's always with someone gorgeous. But if you find out that he does happen to be available...'

'Sure, I'll put in a word,' Charlotte said.

'You're not tempted yourself?' Lisa asked.

Yes. Not that she was going to admit it. 'I'm quite happy breakfasting with Pandora,' Charlotte said with a smile.

James couldn't help overhearing the very last bit of the conversation. Pandora? Who was Pandora? Charlotte's sister? Her flatmate? Or...

He considered whether Pandora might be Charlotte's partner, then dismissed the idea. No, Charlotte didn't seem the type.

And if she was talking about having breakfast with a friend or her sister or something, not her partner...did that mean she was available?

He turned away, cross with himself. It was ridiculous he was even thinking about it. He had no intention of dating someone he had to work with so closely. Even if she was incredibly pretty, with that silky blonde hair pulled back in another French pleat, the slightest hint of a retroussé nose and a perfect rosebud mouth.

His body reacted instantly to the idea of that mouth exploring his body, that hair loose and trailing over his skin, and he groaned inwardly. For pity's sake. He barely knew her. She'd been reserved with him so far—except when they'd been discussing a patient, when she'd seemed to relax with him.

Plus she'd just told Lisa point blank that she wasn't interested in him.

He needed to get a grip, and keep his mind focused firmly on work. After the mess of his marriage, he wasn't prepared to offer anyone more than a casual relationship, and he knew without asking that Charlotte Walker was definitely not the kind of woman who'd accept that kind of deal. Which meant she was off limits. He found her attractive—very attractive—but he wasn't going to act on that attraction.

'Sorry about that,' Charlotte said, returning to James's side.

He smiled. 'No worries.'

'By the way, do I introduce you to the Freemans as Mr Alexander?'

'James,' he said. 'It's tough enough for parents, seeing their children go into Theatre, without them having to worry about formality and protocol, and what the difference is between calling someone "Doctor" and calling them "Mister".'

Her thoughts exactly. 'Good. And you're OK with Daisy calling you Dr James?'

'She can call me whatever makes her feel comfortable.' He paused. 'What does she call you?'

'Dr Charlotte.'

'Not Dr Charlie?'

'Nobody calls me Charlie,' she said quietly. 'Ever.'

'Noted,' he said.

It wasn't the strict truth. Michael had called her Charlie. But after she'd left Liverpool, she'd made a conscious decision to stick to her full name. Anyone who tried a diminutive was gently but firmly guided back to the name she preferred. Not that she intended to explain any of that to James. That was on a strictly need-to-know basis.

When they reached Daisy's cubicle, Charlotte greeted Leslie and Gary Freeman warmly, then sat on the edge of Daisy's bed and gave her a cuddle. 'Hello, gorgeous.'

'Hello, Dr Charlotte.' The little girl gave her a beaming smile and hugged her back.

'I've brought someone special to see you,' Charlotte said. 'This is Dr James. He's the doctor who's going to fix your heart this morning.'

'Hello, Dr James,' Daisy said shyly.

Charlotte introduced James quickly to Daisy's parents.

'I'm sorry I wasn't in yesterday,' James said, 'but I wanted to see you before the operation. I know Charlotte's already taken you through what's going to happen today, but it's a lot to take in. If you want us to go over anything again, or there's anything else you'd like to know, just ask. That's what I'm here for.'

'Charlotte said that you'll close the hole either with stitches or a patch,' Gary said.

James nodded. 'I've studied Daisy's X-rays and the echo-cardiogram results—they're the ones that show us how her blood moves through her heart—and in Daisy's case I'm going to use a patch. The whole thing should take about three hours, and she'll be on a bypass machine while I'm closing the hole in her heart.'

'You met Carlo yesterday—he's the one who'll be looking after the bypass machine, and he's getting everything ready for Daisy now,' Charlotte said. 'And you remember Fran, the an-aesthetist?' At their nod, she said, 'Fran should be down to see us in about five minutes.'

'Are you and Poppy both ready for your big day, then?' James asked Daisy.

Daisy nodded. 'Poppy had a operation, too. Look.' She showed him the scar on the doll's chest.

'Wow. Shall I tell you a secret?' James asked conspiratori-ally.

The little girl's blue eyes widened. 'What?'

'My stitches are much neater than that,' James confided in

a whisper. 'So you'll only have a little scar, and it'll fade as you get bigger.'

Daisy swallowed. 'Is it going to hurt?'

'The scar? No. If you're worried about the operation, you'll be asleep when I fix your heart, so it won't hurt you at all while I do it,' James said. 'You might feel a little bit sore when you wake up afterwards, but all you have to do is tell Mummy or Daddy or one of the nurses, and they'll make it better.'

'Like when I falled over and hurted my knee,' Daisy said.

'Exactly like that. And I'll tell you another secret. A kiss better always helps.'

Daisy smiled. 'Do you like having a kiss better?'

'Yes, I do,' James said.

Charlotte was shocked at the image that flashed into her head. Of herself kissing James. Crazy. The surgeon didn't need kissing better, and she had no intention of kissing him in any case. Though the idea of it still made her skin heat and her pulse rate speed up a notch. She only hoped that mind-reading wasn't part of his skill set.

'Shall we play with Poppy for a minute, Daisy?' James said. 'I think you need to take her temperature, to check she's not too hot.'

Daisy pretended to take the doll's temperature. 'No, she's just right.'

'Excellent. Now it's my turn—can I check you?'

Daisy nodded; James checked her temperature and indicated the results to Charlotte, who noted it on the chart. 'Like Poppy—just right,' he pronounced.

In the same way, he did the rest of the medical checks to reassure himself that Daisy was fit for surgery, and Daisy was clearly delighted that this tall, handsome man was happy to play dolls with her.

Charlotte had to admit that she was impressed. James had put the little girl at ease very quickly, and as a consequence her parents were more relaxed, too.

'Right, then, Little Miss Beautiful,' James said, smiling at her. 'I have to go and put my doctor's stuff on now. Dr Charlotte here will give you some special medicine that'll make you feel all sleepy, as if your mummy's been reading you your favourite bedtime story, and I'll see you in Theatre very soon.' He ruffled her hair, then turned to Leslie and Gary. 'I'll leave you in Charlotte's very capable hands. As soon as we're out of Theatre, I'll come and see you, and take you to see Daisy in Intensive Care. I know it's easy for me to say, but please try not to worry. She's going to feel so much better in a couple of days.'

Once James had left, Charlotte stayed with the Freemans while Fran arranged Daisy's premeds, and walked with them to Theatre.

Leslie and Gary both made an effort to be smiley and brave for their daughter as she was wheeled through the door, blowing her kisses goodbye, but Leslie was in tears the second that the doors closed behind the trolley.

'Hey, it's going to be fine.' Charlotte held her close and stroked her hair. 'James Alexander has a brilliant reputation as a surgeon. Daisy's in the best hands possible.'

'But isn't he new?' Leslie dragged in a breath. 'The nurses were talking about him last night.'

'New to the hospital, yes, but not new to surgery. He's been working in London at one of the biggest children's hospitals, and he's got lots of experience. Honestly, Leslie, Daisy's in really good hands.'

When Leslie's sobs had died down, Charlotte gave her a last hug. 'Waiting's the worst part. Come and sit in the relatives' room and I'll get you a coffee. Have either of you eaten today?'

'No,' Gary admitted. 'We couldn't face anything this morning.'

'You need to keep your strength up, too. You don't want your blood sugar dipping and making you feel rough on top of all the worry.' Charlotte took them back to the ward, settled them in the relatives' room, and made coffee for them as well as a pile of toast. 'I've had a word with the nursing staff. They said to help yourself to whatever you need in the kitchen. They know you're here, and I'll make sure the team in Theatre know where you are, too. As soon as there's any news, James will come and see you.' She patted Leslie's hand. 'I'm in clinic from a quarter past nine for the rest of the morning, but if you need me just ask one of the nurses to bleep me and I'll be straight with you, OK? And as soon as I've finished clinic, I'll come up and see you.'

'Thanks, Charlotte.' Leslie mopped her eyes. 'I'm sorry. I should pull myself together.'

'Anyone in your shoes would be doing exactly the same thing. But, as James said, hold onto the fact that she's going to be so much better in a few days.'

Charlotte was scrupulous in paying attention to her patients during her clinic, doing routine echos and ECGs, but she was also very aware of the time. As the morning ticked on and she still hadn't been bleeped, she began to worry. She knew that the operation usually took three hours, so she should have heard something by now.

Which meant either something was very badly wrong, or James hadn't bothered keeping her in the picture.

She just prayed it was the latter.

When she'd seen her last patient, she headed for her office to ring Intensive Care and find out if Daisy was back from Theatre and how she was doing. The phone rang as she was about to pick it up; suppressing a sigh, she answered. 'Cardio, Charlotte speaking.'

'Charlotte, it's Dave in Emergency. I know you usually do kids, but I can't get hold of Tim and I've got a patient here with bradycardia. I really don't like the look of the ECG. Could you do us a favour and take a look?'

No, I need to find out how my patient is doing, Charlotte thought. But then she pulled herself together. As much as she wanted to find out about Daisy, she was here to do a job. And she was needed in the emergency department. 'Sure. I'm on my way.'

As she left the department, she called into Steffie's office. 'Tim's not responding to his bleep, so Emergency called me—so you know where I am if anyone needs me.'

'Rightio. Do you want me to let this afternoon's clinic know you'll be running late?'

'I should be back in time. But if you can do me a huge favour—I still haven't heard how Daisy Freeman's doing. Obviously Mr Alexander was too busy to get a message through, so can you ask Barb to find out for me, please?' Barbara, the departmental secretary, was an organisational wizard. 'And I'd appreciate it if she can let Leslie and Gary know where I am, too. They're probably in the Paediatric ITU right now with Daisy, though I left them in the relatives' room before clinic this morning.'

'I'll get Barb onto it,' Steffie said. 'Do you want me to bring you a sandwich back from the canteen?'

'Please—and I promise I'll grab five minutes to eat it.'

'You'd better.' Steffie's voice was stern, but there was a twinkle in her eyes.

'Bleep me if you need me,' Charlotte said, smiling back at her, and left the department.

CHAPTER FOUR

WHEN Charlotte came back to the cardiology unit from the emergency department, she went to find Steffie. 'Dave's sending a patient up. Is Tim back from wherever he was, so I can tell him what I've done?'

'He's gone home with a bug. Barb's rearranging his clinic for this afternoon.'

Charlotte knew what that meant. They were short-staffed and she'd need to do Tim's rounds. 'OK. I've done the admission forms. Mrs Harvey was bradycardic—Dave and I think she might be hypothyroid and it hasn't been picked up, so we've sent off some bloods. She didn't respond to atropine, so I've put in a temporary pacing wire to get her heart back to a normal rhythm.'

'I'll keep an eye on her, and come and get you if there's a problem.'

Charlotte knew that Steffie was experienced enough to spot a problem quickly, and could tell exactly when to deal with it herself and when to call one of the cardiologists. 'Thanks, Steffie. I'll come and see her again when my clinic's finished, and I'll do Tim's round then as well. Did Barb manage to find out how Daisy's doing?'

'Still in Theatre.'

Charlotte winced. 'That's really not good. Do we know what the problem is?'

'No, but James has a real reputation.'

Charlotte bit her lip. 'I hope he lives up to it.' His reputation as an excellent surgeon, she meant—not the one he had as a playboy.

'I'm sure he will. Stop worrying, and you make sure you take a break before you go into clinic, OK? Here.' She handed Charlotte a packet of sandwiches.

'Thanks, you're an angel. How much do I owe you?'

The call light flashed outside one of the rooms, and Steffie waved a dismissive hand. 'Settle up with me later. I have to run. And make sure you take a break!'

'Course I will,' Charlotte fibbed, and bolted her sandwich as she checked through the list for her afternoon clinic.

Although she paid scrupulous attention to each of her patients, she looked at her pager between every appointment, just in case there was news. Nothing.

Her last patient was twelve-year-old Ellis Martyn, who was accompanied by his mother, Judy. The teachers at high school had picked up on Ellis being very short of breath in PE lessons; the GP had confirmed a heart murmur and referred him to Charlotte.

'What you have is something called Ebstein's anomaly,' she explained. 'It's quite a rare heart condition, but the important thing is that we can do something to help you.'

'So I'm going to be really ill?' Ellis asked.

She smiled. 'I should jolly well hope not!' She did a quick sketch on the pad before her. 'See this bit here? This is the tricuspid valve. It separates the chamber of your heart that receives blood from the body and the chamber of your heart that pumps the blood to your lungs so it can be oxygenated. In your case, Ellis, the valve's situated too low in your heart and it leaks backwards. That means some of the unoxygenated blood goes into your body instead of to your lungs—so that's why you're tired a lot of the time, why you get a bit short of breath and why sometimes your mouth looks a bit blue.' Gently, she took his hand and turned it palm down. 'See, your nail beds are a bit blue as well. When I did the test measuring the amount of oxygen in your blood, it told me the oxygen levels were too low; the X-rays told me your heart's definitely enlarged; and the echo showed me that the valve was leaking. Now, you said your heart started racing every so often?'

The boy nodded.

'When I hooked you up to the machine so I could see how your heart beats, the rhythm seemed fine, so I'd like you to take a portable recorder home with you and come back and see me in about a week. I'll show you and your mum how to attach it and do the recording, and then I can see how the rhythm of your heart changes.'

'What's going to happen next?' Judy asked.

'Right now, I'm going to put Ellis on antibiotics. It's not going to cure you,' she warned, 'but it should prevent you picking up an infection that'll affect your endocardium—that's the lining in the chambers of your heart.'

Judy was scribbling away in a notepad, and Charlotte reached over to squeeze her hand. 'Judy, there's a lot to take in and I appreciate you have a lot of questions. I can give you a leaflet to take away with you, and I'm also going to write you a proper letter, explaining everything, so you don't have to worry about taking notes. It'll be in the post first thing tomorrow morning, and I'll send a copy to your family doctor as well. But I do think we're looking at surgery, so I want to talk to James Alexander, our cardiac surgeon. He'll need to repair the valve so it stops leaking and makes Ellis well again.'

Ellis looked worried. 'Is it going to hurt?'

'You'll be a bit sore afterwards,' Charlotte said gently, 'but the important thing is that we do something to help you.'

'How did he get it? And is he going to…?' Judy stopped, clearly not wanting to ask the question in front of her son.

Charlotte squeezed her hand again. 'He was born with it. In Ellis's case, it's relatively mild, because it wasn't picked up before. Your new GP sent you both to see me because of Ellis's symptoms, so my guess is that the breathlessness and blueness round his lips have got worse over the years.' She smiled at them. 'The good news is that if Ebstein's isn't diagnosed until you're a year old, you have a good chance of having a normal life. Ellis is twelve, so he's got an even better chance of living a completely normal life.'

'But he's going to have heart surgery…'

'Open heart surgery.' Charlotte nodded. 'Very likely. What I'd like is for you to come back next week and talk to the surgeon with me.'

James. Gorgeous, hotshot James who hadn't bothered telling her how her patient was. But it wasn't the Martyns' fault, so she wasn't going to let them see her anger.

'If the surgeon agrees with me that Ellis needs surgery, now's a goodish time as Ellis is relatively well and the school holidays start very soon. If we do the op in the first week of the holidays, it'll give him a few weeks to recover before the new term starts.'

'What about exercise? Should he stop doing anything?' Judy asked.

Charlotte shook her head. 'Do what you're comfortable with. I'd say steer clear of really intense, competitive sports, but regular, gentle exercise is good for you. Walking, swimming, cycling…' She smiled at Ellis. 'Provided you're not going for the sprint record, that is!'

As soon as the clinic had finished, Charlotte went in search of Steffie. 'Any news of Daisy?'

'Not yet.'

Charlotte sighed. 'Then I'll check Mrs Harvey and do Tim's round. I hope we've got cover for tomorrow.'

'Yes—Barb's sorted it.'

'And let me settle up with you for that sandwich.'

Steffie rolled her eyes. 'Charlotte, it was a sandwich, and you've done the same for me plenty of times. Stop fussing.'

Charlotte had finished the rounds and was going through the paperwork in her office when James turned up, carrying two paper cups of coffee with lids. She just about resisted the urge to yell at him and ask him what the hell he was playing at, not keeping her in touch with the results of Daisy's operation; and it annoyed her that her heart gave that funny little skip as soon as her gaze meshed with his. She didn't react to people like that. Didn't *want* to react to him like that.

She took a deep breath and asked quietly, 'Is Daisy all right?'

'She's fine. Here.' He passed her one of the cups of coffee.

She took a sip. It was just how she liked it, strong with just a dash of milk. 'Thank you,' she said. 'It's the first chance I've had for a hot drink all day. How did you know how I take my coffee?'

'I asked Steffie—and I owed you a coffee from yesterday, before you protest.'

'You don't owe me anything.' Including, it seemed, the courtesy of letting her know how her patient was getting on.

He sighed. 'Look, you're the paediatric cardiologist and I'm the paediatric heart surgeon. We're going to have to work together, whether we like it or not—and I for one would much rather have smooth working relationships. It's better for the patients.'

Charlotte felt herself flush. 'Rebuke accepted.'

'It wasn't meant to be a rebuke.' He dragged a hand through his hair. 'I think we're getting off on the wrong foot.' He frowned as she laughed. 'What?'

'Your hair's all messy now.'

'And?'

'And I'm waiting for you to whip out the comb and the mirror.'

'I'm not that vain. Well, not *quite*,' he amended. 'Anyway, I wanted to keep you in the loop about Daisy.'

'Who was supposed to be out of Theatre more than four hours ago,' she said pointedly.

'There were complications.'

She could see shadows under his eyes, and panicked. Despite his reassurance earlier, now she wasn't so sure. 'What sort of complications?'

'May I?' James gestured to the chair by her desk.

'Help yourself.'

He sprawled in the chair and set his coffee on her desk. 'The op was a success, but she arrested in the middle of surgery twice—that's why I'm late. Obviously she's settled in ITU now and Leslie and Gary are by her bed.'

'Thanks. I'll go and see them. My reports can wait.'

'Leave it a few minutes,' he said softly. 'She's still sedated, and I told them we won't be waking her up properly until tomorrow morning.'

It was standard procedure after open heart surgery. It meant that the child was on a ventilator that would breathe for her, and that reduced the work her heart had to do so she could rest properly.

'So how's your afternoon been?' he asked.

'Pretty busy,' she admitted. 'The emergency department needed me because Tim—he's the other cardiac registrar— went home with a bug.'

'So you do adults as well as children?'

'Not usually—I do the kids and Tim does the adults. But we can cover each other's patients, obviously, when we have to. And I do have a patient I want to talk to you about in the next few days—Ellis has Ebstein's, and I think we're looking at valve replacement. The ECG didn't show any sign of tachycardia, so I've sent him home with a portable recorder to see what it picks up. But the results from the echo are pretty clear—the valve's leaking. I've made an appointment for them to come back next week, and I think you need to be in on the consultation, as the surgeon.'

'Sure. We'll synchronise diaries.'

'Thanks.'

Clearly Charlotte was very dedicated, James thought. She didn't seem to bat an eyelid about doing a colleague's rounds: she just got on with it. She was quiet and hard-working, so different from the women in his life—even his mother was a society sophisticate who spent her time partying and shopping. Whereas Charlotte Walker was an oasis of calm. Funny, he'd always been one for the bright lights and glitz, but right now he found himself yearning for calm. And Charlotte fascinated him because he didn't have a clue about what made her tick. 'What made you choose cardiology?' he asked abruptly.

She looked surprised, but then she shrugged, as if she'd decided it wasn't really a personal question. 'Originally, I was going to specialise in paediatrics. While I was training we had a blue baby and lost her; it really got to me, and I ended up reading up lots on the subject. I wanted to make a difference, so I decided to go into cardiology. And I tend to work on the paediatric cases, so I get the best of both worlds.' She paused. 'What about you?'

James could have put some spin on it, but he knew that she'd guess straight away that he was being smooth. He didn't want her to think him a liar, so he decided to be honest. 'Not quite so noble, I'm afraid. For me, it was a toss-up between cardiac surgery and brain surgery, but cardiac was the more competitive discipline at the time.'

'And you like to be seen as the best.'

He gave her what he hoped was a disarming smile. 'Shocking, isn't it?'

'You're shameless.'

'No,' he corrected, 'I'm honest.'

She made a noncommittal noise. 'Thanks for letting me know what happened. I think I'd better go up and see the Freemans now.' She waved her hand at the papers on her desk. 'Tonight's post has already gone, so it doesn't matter if I do them later tonight now. They'll be ready for tomorrow.'

He raised an eyebrow. 'You'll be working late, then.'

'I'm not going to leave my patients—or their parents—waiting for reassurance any longer than I have to. Anyway, Tim would've done the same for me if I'd been hit by a virus.'

'Look, I was three hours longer in Theatre than I expected to be. I had to reschedule some appointments and I have reports to write,' he said. 'So I'm going to be working late tonight, too. Why don't we have dinner together?'

'Thanks, but no.'

He stared at her. That was it? Just 'no'? No explanation? 'You're already having dinner with someone tonight?' he guessed.

She shook her head.

'Then why won't you have dinner with me?'

'Because,' she said, 'I don't think we'd like the same sort of places.'

'Try me. Show me where you like to eat in St Piran.'

'Thanks, but I'd rather not.' Still calm, quiet, but very firm.

James couldn't remember the last time he'd been turned down. And it stung. But there was more to it than that: since meeting Charlotte the previous day, he hadn't been able to stop thinking about her. Right now, she was polite, sweet and super-smiley—and he had the feeling that she'd just stuck an enormous glass wall between them. And he had no idea why.

'Would it help,' he asked, 'if I said that I'm new around here and I'm trying very hard to make a new friend, not asking you out on a date?'

The wariness in her eyes was quickly masked. 'A friend.'

'Uh-huh. I'm paying, seeing as it's my idea, but if it makes you feel better, you can pay next time.'

She was silent for so long that he thought he'd blown it. And then she nodded. 'As friends.'

'Good.' He scooped his coffee cup off her desk and stood up. 'I'll be in my office. Come and get me when you've seen the Freemans.'

'OK. And, James?'

He paused in the doorway.

This time she gave him a smile that did reach her eyes. A smile that made his heart skip a beat. 'Thanks for the coffee.'

When Charlotte went through to Intensive Care, the Freemans both looked tired and stressed, but slightly less anxious than they'd done that morning.

She hugged both of them. 'I'm so sorry that I didn't come up earlier.'

'That's OK, we got your messages. That lovely lady told us you had to hold the fort.' Leslie shook her head in apparent frustration. 'Sorry, I don't remember her name.'

'Barbara,' Charlotte said gently.

'Sorry, I couldn't think.'

'I'm not surprised. You've had a hell of a day.'

Leslie was trembling. 'To think, we almost lost her.'

Gary put his arm round his wife's shoulders and held her close. 'Hey, she's a fighter, like her mum. She's not going to give up easily and we're definitely not giving up on her.'

They were going through such a rough time, Charlotte thought, and yet they were lucky: they still had each other. They still had a deep love between them to support them through all the worry and the waiting. The kind of love she knew that she'd never experience. Not after Michael.

She pushed the thought away. Ridiculous. She'd made her decision a long time ago and knew it was the right one. This wistfulness just wasn't her. She was a practical, sensible cardiologist and she needed to remember that.

'James was really good. He stayed with us for half an hour, even though he'd been concentrating on our Daisy for so long and he hadn't had a break—he came straight out of Theatre to see us. He must have been worn out, but he never once made us feel we were taking up his time or being a nuisance. He's a lovely man,' Leslie said.

Lovely, maybe. But he was also dangerous. She must've been mad to agree to go out with him tonight—even as friends.

'I'll let you get back to Daisy,' she said. 'I just wanted to come up and see how you were all doing. Remember you can get hold of me any time you're worried—just tell them to bleep me. I'm taking my pager home tonight.'

'Thank you.' Gary hugged her.

Charlotte finished off her paperwork, then headed for James's office. She watched him from the door for a moment; he was concentrating on his report, oblivious to her presence. Without that smile, he was still gorgeous—a fine bone structure, the longest, darkest, sexiest eyelashes she'd ever seen—and when he looked serious like that, his mouth was utterly kissable.

Having dinner with him tonight was a bad idea. Maybe she should back out, saying that she had a headache. And yet part of her wanted to know: what was James really like, behind that glossy exterior? When he'd said he could use a friend, there had been a hint of vulnerability. Something she couldn't put her finger on, but something that she found hard to resist.

She rapped on the door, and he looked up.

'Hi. How were the Freemans?'

'OK. I'm taking my bleeper with me, by the way.'

'Make that two of us,' he said, surprising her. 'I'm starving. Give me two seconds to save this file.' Deftly, he tapped the keys to save his file, log off and switch off the computer.

'So where are we going?' James asked

'There's a pub ten minutes' walk from here. They do the best lasagne in St Piran.'

'I adore lasagne. Good. Is your car in the hospital car park?'

'No, I walked in.'

'So are we going in the right direction for you?'

She had a nasty feeling that he was going to offer to walk her home—and she wasn't quite ready for that. She wasn't really ready to go out with him tonight either. 'It's fine,' she said hastily.

Although the pub was busy, James managed to find them a quiet table. He ordered the same as she did, including a glass of mineral water. 'If you get called back, so will I,' he reminded her, 'and I never drink alcohol if there's a possibility a patient might need me.'

He kept the conversation light, mainly work, and Charlotte found herself relaxing with him. James was good company, full of anecdotes that made her laugh. She couldn't remember the last time she'd enjoyed an evening so much. And when his fingers accidentally brushed against hers as they both reached for their drinks at the same time, she didn't whip her hand away, as she would normally have done. Instead, she actually found herself enjoying the contact.

Which was worrying. And yet exciting, at the same time. There was something about James; she couldn't put her finger on it, but he was…different. Definitely not like Michael. And not like the men she'd dated in the past.

They were halfway through their lasagne when there was a flash. At first, Charlotte thought someone on another table was taking a group photograph, but when the flashes were repeated, James sighed.

'Just ignore it,' he said.

She frowned. 'Ignore what?'

'Paparazzi.' He rolled his eyes. 'Obviously they've worked out where I am. If you don't make a fuss, they take their picture and then they leave you alone.'

She couldn't quite get her head round this. 'The press are following you?'

He shrugged. 'They've done it ever since I was small. My mum was a top model and Dad's a bit of a big noise in the business world, so once my brother and I came along, I guess it was natural for the press to be interested in us, too.'

'People take your photograph and it doesn't bother you?'

'Actually, it does,' he said, 'but if you make a fuss, the paparazzi think there's a story and it blows up out of proportion. So I've learned that you get a quieter life if you just leave it.'

Charlotte frowned. 'So is someone going to print a photograph of you and me together?'

'There might be something in one of the gossip rags.' He shrugged. 'But you and I know we're just colleagues. Everyone at work knows we're colleagues. And the people who read those magazines know that most of the gossip stuff is just that—pure supposition, not fact. So it's not a big deal.'

'Not a big deal?' Charlotte shook her head. 'James, I'm not comfortable with the idea of a photographer following me around.'

'It's not what you signed up for. I know.' He shrugged. 'And I'm sorry. But trust me on this. It'll be a two-day wonder. Then some celeb or other will be caught wearing something a bit indiscreet at the beach, and the attention will all go there.'

'But I'm not going to be doorstepped or anything?'

'Probably not. Though, to be on the safe side, we'll put you in a taxi from the back of the pub and get the cabbie to take you the long way home.' He smiled at her. 'Just forget about them and finish your lasagne.'

She tried, but she had to admit defeat. How could James be so cool about this kind of interference in his life? 'Sorry. I've lost my appetite.'

'I'm sorry, too,' James said, sounding rueful. 'Because the dessert menu looked fabulous. Maybe next time?'

'Maybe,' she said, trying to sound noncommittal.

True to his word, James organised a taxi for her. On the pretext of going to the loo, she slipped out to meet the taxi driver, while James remained in the pub as the focus for the photographer's attention. Just as James had suggested, the cabbie took the long way home, and Charlotte was surprised to discover that James had already paid the fare. Although she didn't like the idea of being in his debt like this, she had a feeling he'd come up with a reason she couldn't argue with.

When Charlotte unlocked her front door, Pandora was waiting for her on the bottom stair; she bent and scooped up the beautiful Burmese blue, and Pandora purred a welcome.

'Sorry I'm late,' she said, closing the front door behind her. 'It's been one of those days.'

Pandora rubbed her cheek against Charlotte's, as if saying that she knew exactly what kind of day Charlotte meant.

Charlotte set her briefcase down on the floor and went through to the kitchen; she sat down at the kitchen table, and the cat curled comfortably on her lap. 'I can't get James Alexander out of my head and that worries me,' she said, making a fuss of the cat. 'I always said I wouldn't get involved again. And yet... There's something about him that makes me want to take a chance.'

Kate Althorp turned the shower on to full and stepped underneath it. At least with the water going, she knew that Jem wouldn't hear her crying.

She was so sick of being brave. But she sure as hell wasn't going to dump how she was feeling on a ten-year-old boy who was feeling even more scared than she was. Which was why she was crying on her own in the shower at nine o'clock in the evening.

She'd told Jem half of it—given that she was going to have to stay in St Piran's for a couple of days, she couldn't exactly not tell him. So she'd explained that she'd found a lump, that she'd been to see the doctor and there was a problem, but just as Jem's face had crumpled, she'd hugged him hard. 'Hey. It's going to be OK. Dr Bower said she was pretty sure all she has to do is take out the lump. I have to stay in for a couple of days, but it's going to be right at the beginning of the summer holidays and you're going to have a really mega-sleepover at Matthew's. Rob says he'll take you both out on your bikes and down to the beach, and you're going to have loads of pizza and ice cream. It's all going to be fine.'

God only knew how she'd found the strength to say it with a smile on her face. And keep back the warning that Rob knew about: that the plan was for a lumpectomy, but things might change. Once she was on the table, and Dr Bower had opened her up and seen what was there around the lump.

And she definitely wasn't going to tell Jem of her fears.

What if it wasn't just one little lump? What if, once she was on the table, Dr Bower found it had already spread to the lymph nodes—or, God forbid, further than that?

What if they hadn't caught it in time?

What if she didn't live to see her boy grow up?

Despite the heat of the water, Kate couldn't stop her teeth chattering. Couldn't stop the waves of fear. There was still so much she wanted to share with Jem. She wanted to see him grow up into the sweet, clever, loving man she knew he'd become. She wanted to be there when he passed his exams at school, teach him to drive, help him fly when he finally wanted to leave the nest. She wanted to be there on his wedding day, seeing him pledge his love to a woman who'd love him all the way back. She wanted to hold his firstborn child, and as she looked into her grandchild's eyes she would remember the moment she'd first held Jem and looked into his eyes.

There were so many things she still wanted to do.

And what if she didn't have the time? What if she never got to share those moments with him, never got the chance to make those precious memories?

She was all he had, as far as Jem was concerned.

Except…she wasn't. Because Jem had a father—a father who still wouldn't recognise him, despite his promise to try. A father who'd walked away from them both after a stupid throw-away comment by a tourist.

Things between her and Nick had been incredibly strained ever since.

But if the worst came to the worst, Jem would need someone to look after him. He'd need a father. Kate dragged in a breath. Jem had to come first. Which meant she had to go and face Nick. Talk to him again. Make sure that, if something happened to her, he'd take care of their son. That he'd look after Jem and love him and be there for him. If he really had to save face and stop tongues wagging in Penhally, he could always say he was being the guardian to the son of an old friend. And then instead of being just 'Uncle Nick', who blew hot and cold, he could be a real father to Jem.

But would Nick see it the same way?

CHAPTER FIVE

ON THE Wednesday morning, Charlotte called into Intensive Care before her shift to see Daisy and her parents. James was already there, and greeted her with a smile. 'Perfect timing. We're going to wake Daisy up shortly,' he said. 'She'll still have a breathing tube in for a little while; once we're happy she's breathing well, we'll take the tube out and give her an oxygen mask, to help ease her back into breathing on her own. Hopefully I'll be able to remove the pacing wires and her chest drains tomorrow, and she'll be back on the children's ward on Friday.'

'It'll be lovely just to hear her chattering,' Leslie said.

'That might be a little while, because she'll have a bit of sore throat,' James warned. 'But encourage her to sip water, little and often. Now, I need a quick word with Charlotte about a couple of patients—do you mind if I just whisk her off into the corridor?'

'Sure,' Gary said with a smile.

Charlotte stepped outside with James.

'Did you get home all right last night without any trouble?' he asked.

'Yes. And thank you for paying for the taxi. You didn't need to do that.'

'Actually, I did. If it hadn't been for the press, you would've walked home.'

'True. But it was still nice of you.' She paused. 'Maybe I could buy you lunch today.'

He raised an eyebrow. 'Are you asking me out?'

Yes. No. A dozen replies skittered round her head, but nothing would come out of her mouth.

This was *awful*. She was never indecisive like this.

Now he'd think she was a complete idiot.

James reached out to stroke her cheek with the backs of his fingers; his touch and his smile made her knees go weak.

'I'm teasing, Charlotte. Lunch would be great. And, actually, I have a favour to ask.'

'What sort of favour?'

'I hear you're fitting a pacemaker today. Do you mind if I come and sit in?'

She blinked. 'Aren't you in Theatre? I thought you had another ASD to fix?'

'I did, but I wasn't happy with my patient's obs. I think she's cutting a tooth, but I'm not risking it in case the temperature's caused by something else—I've put it back a fortnight to give her a chance either to get over any infection or cut the tooth. I have a free slot, so it's a good opportunity to see the cath lab here in action.'

She was relieved that he'd gone back to a common-sense, professional approach. Something she could do, too, without making a fool of herself. 'As long as my patient and his mum don't mind,' she said.

'And he's your first patient this morning?'

'Yes. I'm going to see him on the children's ward after I've talked to the Freemans.'

'I might as well join you.'

She had a quick catch-up with the Freemans, gave them the book she'd bought to cheer Daisy up—about a cat just like her own—and, on the way to the children's ward, she filled James in about Danny, her twelve-year-old patient with an irregular heartbeat. She gave his tie a sidelong glance. 'I'm glad you don't have the teddies today, because I think Danny might be a bit sarcastic about it.'

James laughed. 'I was a teenage boy once, too.'

'Don't come in with me. It'll make them feel pressured,' Charlotte said, 'and if they say no, I'm not going to push them.'

'Sure.'

On the ward, Danny was wearing a hospital gown and was looking fed up with waiting. After she'd greeted him and his mother and made sure they were both happy with what was going to happen that morning, she asked, 'Danny, Maria, would you mind if my colleague sits in on the procedure? He's new to the hospital and wants to see this side of the cardio unit in action.'

'Fine by me,' Danny said with a shrug.

'Me, too,' Maria said.

'Excellent. I'll just go and get him.'

When she stepped into the corridor, she wasn't surprised to discover James was flirting with Lisa. 'Sorry to interrupt,' she said coolly, 'but if you want to come with us to the cath lab, James, it's fine with Danny and Maria.'

'That's great. See you later, Lisa.' James gave the junior doctor a dazzling smile, which made Charlotte feel distinctly out of sorts—and cross with herself for feeling that way—and then walked with her to Danny's bedside.

She introduced him swiftly. 'This is my colleague James, the cardiac surgeon.'

'That's James, as in Bond,' James said with a grin.

'You are *such* a flanneller,' Charlotte said.

'Hey. I have the watch to prove it.' He pulled the cuff of his shirt back just far enough to show Danny his watch.

'Wow, that's so cool,' Danny said, his eyes widening.

Maria, too, seemed impressed by James. Well, that was par for the course. James seemed to be able to charm practically anyone female.

'And I've got a pilot's licence,' James added.

'Really?' Danny looked seriously impressed.

Charlotte groaned. 'Oh, for goodness' sake. Next thing, he's going to tell you he's got an Aston Martin.'

'I have. It's a DBS V12,' James said with a grin. 'A silver one.'

'No *way*,' Danny said, sounding delighted. 'Can I go for a ride in it?'

'If it's OK with your mum, sure you can.'

Charlotte folded her arms. 'Enough of the Bond stuff, guys. We're doing real bionic stuff here.'

'For your information, Dr Walker, the Aston Martin's real,' James said. 'I'll prove it—I'll give you a lift home in it some time.'

'You can give *me* a lift home, if you like,' Danny suggested with a beaming smile.

'Not tonight, he can't,' Charlotte said. 'I want you in where we can keep an eye on you and make sure that it's all gone well.'

James and his Aston Martin. She really wasn't sure whether he was teasing or telling the truth; given that his watch was exactly what he'd said it was, she had a feeling that it was the latter. Completely flashy.

But at least it had taken the worry out of Danny's eyes.

'I'm utterly starving. Mum wouldn't even let me have a drink of water after eight o'clock last night, and I'm absolutely desperate for a cheeseburger with extra tomato ketchup. The only thing I've had today was antibiotics, and that was disgusting!' Danny complained.

Charlotte laughed. 'That's to make sure you don't pick up an infection. And I really hate to tell you this, but you've got an antibiotic for lunch *and* for dinner.'

Danny groaned. 'Oh, that's *so* unfair.'

She smiled. 'If you're good, I might let you have some food as well.'

'I'll be good. Really good. Scouts' honour,' Danny said quickly.

She ruffled his hair. 'I know. Now, you're OK with the fact it's an overnight stay and tomorrow you need a day's rest?'

'Sure.'

'The op's going to take about an hour. We went through it last time, but I know it's a lot to take in so I'll quickly run through what I'm going to do when we get to the cath lab.'

Once they were settled, she showed them the pacemaker. 'Basically, it's a battery and electronic circuit sealed in metal. The circuit takes energy from the battery and turns it into electrical impulses; the impulses go down an electrode to your heart and make it beat in the right kind of rhythm. It works "on demand", so if your heartbeat goes irregular it'll kick in, but if your heart's beating normally it won't interfere. It's also like a tiny computer, because it stores information that I can retrieve in a machine and tells me how well your heart and the pace-maker are working.'

'So it's really bionic,' Danny said. 'Cool.'

She smiled at him. 'I'm going to fit a dual chamber pace-maker—that just means it has two leads. Now, you're right-handed, yes?'

'Yes.'

'Then I'll put this on your left-hand side. OK—can you take your top off for me?' The boy was still smooth-chested, so she didn't have to shave him, but she cleansed the area she was going to work with, covered him with sterile drapes and got him ready for the op. Swiftly, she put an IV line in. 'I'm going to give you the anaesthetic now. You'll feel a bit hot and then you'll feel a bit woozy. I'm not going to hurt you, but you might feel as if I'm pulling you a bit. Are you ready?'

'Ready,' Danny said.

She gave him the anaesthetic. 'OK, Danny?' she asked. At his nod, she said, 'Good boy. It's not going to be long now.'

James watched Charlotte working: how she made a small incision just below Danny's collarbone and threaded an electrode through a vein in his shoulder. She guided it into the correct chamber of his heart, using the X-ray screen to show her where the electrode was going, then secured it in position. After that, she connected the electrode to the pacemaker, cut a small pocket between the skin and the muscle of Danny's chest, slid the pacemaker inside and closed up the pocket.

James was impressed by how deft her hands were and how neat the sutures were; Charlotte was very, very good with her hands. He could just imagine those hands stroking his skin, and it made him shiver.

Bad.

Very bad.

He was supposed to be concentrating on work and staying single, not letting himself get distracted by a colleague.

But he found Charlotte irresistible. Not just because she was beautiful, but because she seemed completely unaware of it. Charlotte wasn't like the woman who'd stomped all over his heart and made sure the cameras saw her doing it; she was kind and sweet. And he really, *really* wanted her.

He caught her gaze and saw a momentary flare of heat, quickly damped down again.

So it was mutual.

Good.

'When the anaesthetic wears off, is it going to hurt? Like when I broke my arm ice-skating?' Danny asked.

'There will be a bit of bruising around the site, but it shouldn't be too bad,' Charlotte reassured him, 'and we'll give you painkillers. You won't even be able to see the pace-maker, because it'll be hidden by your muscle.'

Danny, clearly making an effort to joke to mask his fears, said, 'I always knew I was a muscle man at heart. And now I'm a bionic muscle man.'

'You certainly are,' Charlotte said. 'I want to check your pacemaker now to be sure it's working, so I'm going to put this magnet on your skin. This will pull a switch inside the pacemaker to make it work and send electrical impulses into your heart, and I can programme it with this computer. You might feel your heart beating faster, but don't worry—just tell me what you're feeling, when you're feeling it.'

She checked that the pacemaker was running properly, listening to what Danny said and adjusting it accordingly. 'Yep, this will do.' She removed the magnet. 'Right, all done. You've been absolutely brilliant.' She smiled at him. 'Don't do any vigorous exercise for three weeks in case you move it out of position, but try and keep your shoulder mobile. You need to do some gentle movements on the side where I fitted the pacemaker; the physio will show you what to do a bit later, when you're back on the ward.'

'Can I still play footy?' Danny asked.

She glanced at James; to her relief, he picked up the unspoken message that this might be something that was better coming from someone who played football and understood just how much of a wrench it would be to stop playing. 'Contact sports are out, I'm afraid,' James explained. 'You need to avoid getting hit or kicked on the area around your pacemaker—so I'd avoid football, rugby and kickboxing.'

'And I suppose tennis and cricket have a risk of me being whacked, too,' Danny said glumly.

'I'm afraid so.'

The boy looked devastated. 'So what does that leave me? Walking the dog? Or is that banned, too?'

'Walking's fine. Or athletics. Swimming. And I'd wear a pad over the area where your pacemaker is, to be safe.'

'Oh.' He digested the news. 'Am I still allowed to kiss my girlfriend?'

Maria looked shocked. 'Danny, since when do you have a girlfriend? And how come I don't know about her?'

'Mu-u-um, I'm not going to tell you, am I? That's gross!' The boy shuffled on his seat. 'It's not as if I'm having *sex* with her.'

'I should hope not!'

'We just hold hands and kiss, that's all,' Danny said. 'It's cool. Really.'

'Hmm. We'll talk later,' Maria said, clearly not wanting to embarrass her son by discussing it in front of the doctors.

'Can I still use my games console?' Danny asked, looking worried.

'Yes. Pacemakers are built so they shouldn't interfere with equipment. You don't have to worry about avoiding the microwave or a computer—though you do need to make sure you keep your mobile phone away from the pacemaker. Use your right ear as it's on your left, and don't put your phone in your left pocket. And you also need to carry your pacemaker registration card with you in case you set off security system in airports or shops.' She grinned. 'It has been known to happen.'

'So I can use my games console on the ward?'

'Provided you take things easy and don't use any wireless connections.'

'Or my mobile phone.' He nodded. 'Mum's already told me about it interfering with stuff.'

Maria rolled her eyes. 'Believe it or not, Danny, I was your age once.'

'Tell you a secret, Danny,' James said. 'Mothers *always* know best.'

'You can go back to the ward whenever you feel like it,' Charlotte said. 'I'll come and see you later, and then give you an X-ray tomorrow before I let you out.'

'Cool.' Danny smiled at her.

'You might be a bit sore, but just tell the nurse if you are, OK? And I meant it about the antibiotics—it's to make sure you don't get any infections. When you get home, if you notice any redness, swelling or discharge, or you get a fever, see your family doctor or come back to us straight away.'

'What about his stitches? When do they need to come out?' Maria asked.

'They're dissolvable ones,' James said. 'Before you go tomorrow, we'll give you a letter to take to your GP.'

'But you'll be back in a month to see us, to check everything's OK, and then in three months' time, and eventually you'll go down to just an annual check to make sure the battery's still working,' Charlotte added.

When Danny returned to the ward, James said, 'I'm impressed. I like the way you work.'

She inclined her head in acknowledgement. 'Thank you.'

'I think it's a good idea, too, to see how each other works. Maybe you'd like to sit in on one of my operations.'

'Maybe.'

'How about the Ebstein's case you were telling me about— Ellis, wasn't it?'

'Yes.'

'Good.' He smiled at her. 'By the way, I really was telling the truth about my car—I cycled in today, but the car's in my garage. I'm dying to explore the Cornish coast. How about you come with me on Saturday and show me around a bit?'

It was tempting. Seriously tempting. She got as far as starting to say yes—and then she remembered what had happened in the pub and backed off. 'Sorry. No can do.'

'You were about to say yes.'

'I was,' she admitted, 'but I don't want to be dragged through the press, James.' She wanted to keep her private life just that: *private*. 'I'm sorry. I don't do flash. I'm not like the beauty queens you date.'

'That's true, though probably not in the way you're thinking,' James said. 'How about if I say just as friends?'

Friends. She tried to think of him sitting in her garden, with Pandora draped round his neck, and failed; apart from the fact that Pandora was even more wary of men than Charlotte herself was, she couldn't picture James doing anything so domesticated. Couldn't picture him in old jeans and a faded black

T-shirt and bare feet. He was definitely the formal designer suit, handmade shirt and Italian shoe type.

And it would be much, *much* safer for her if she said no. Keeping temptation well out of arm's reach.

'I'm sorry, James. But thank you for asking,' she said politely.

'Is it true?' Steffie asked, coming into the staff kitchen later that day and looking at Charlotte with her arms folded.

'Is what true?'

'That James Alexander asked you out and you turned him down.'

'Mmm,' she said, concentrating on pouring hot water onto the instant coffee in her mug.

'Why, Charlotte? He's gorgeous. And he's a good doctor.'

True on both counts. Not that she was going to admit it. The last thing she wanted was for Steffie to start matchmaking. 'Whatever,' she drawled.

'Charlotte, just about all the single females in this hospital would be desperate to swap places with you and say yes. Why on earth did you turn him down?'

The truth would involve explanations she didn't want to give. Instead, she said, 'He's too flashy for me. So, now we've cleared that up, can I go back to making my coffee and writing up my notes?'

'You're mad. Utterly mad.' Steffie shook her head.

James, who had been near enough to the open kitchen door to overhear half the conversation, made a swift exit. The last thing he wanted was for Charlotte to find him eavesdropping. Not that it had been intentional.

So Charlotte thought he was too flashy.

OK, so he'd overdone it a bit with the James Bond stuff to help stop Danny feeling nervous. But she'd taken it too seriously. He really wasn't that bad...was he?

But as he left the hospital that night, he had to acknowledge that Charlotte had a point. He might be cycling home, but it wasn't on just any old bicycle. His was a seriously expensive bike, the latest model with a very lightweight carbon composite frame and carbon forks and top-notch components. He was going back to his rented town-house—which had a sea view and was in the most expensive part of St Piran. And he really did own an Aston Martin…along with several other cars, back in London.

Maybe, he thought, Charlotte had been hurt by an ex who had focused too much on what people earned and not enough on what someone was like inside.

Maybe what he needed to do was find out what made her tick.

And then maybe she'd let him get close enough to prove to her that he wasn't as vain and thoughtless as she clearly believed him to be. And to teach her that just because you had a serious job, it didn't mean that you weren't allowed to have any fun.

CHAPTER SIX

ON THURSDAY, Danny's X-ray was completely clear. Charlotte was relieved, because one of the most likely complications with fitting a pacemaker was a pneumothorax, where the chest cavity filled with air. Fixable, admittedly, but painful, and she'd rather that the boy didn't have to go through it. 'It's all fine, so you can go home today,' she told him with a smile. 'And I'll see you next month.'

She and James were both too busy in clinic that day for their paths to cross, but on Friday, just after Daisy was transferred to the children's ward, he sauntered into her office.

'Can I have a word?' he asked.

'Sure. Do you need me to get a file out?'

'No. It's not work exactly.'

James was aware the very second Charlotte put the barrier up: a flicker of wariness in her eyes, followed by a super-bright smile. But he pressed on. 'It's about Tuesday night. The quiz. I'm on the surgeons' team.'

'Uh-huh.'

'And Steffie said the other day that you're head of the cardio team.'

'Yes,' she admitted.

'Then I'd like to make a bet with you. If my team beats yours then you go out to dinner with me.'

'And if mine beats yours,' she said, 'then you leave me alone.'

'Agreed.' He inclined his head. 'That's settled. Have a nice weekend, Charlotte.'

'You, too.'

James strolled out of her office, cool and calm. But inside he was jumping up and down and cheering. Charlotte was bright—very bright—but so was he. And he had no intention of losing. Especially now the stakes were high enough to give him a challenge.

He dropped in to see Jack on Friday night, to have a beer. Jack's father, Nick, had come over to see the children and was apparently helping Alison with bathtime, judging from the fine baritone James could hear floating through the bathroom window.

'So how have you settled in?' Jack asked. 'Sorry I haven't had a chance to catch up with you, but you know what it's like in surgery.'

'Busy, busy, busy,' James said with a grin. 'Which is just how I like it. No, it's fine. And I must say, I'm impressed with your cousin. She's very good at her job.'

'She's brilliant with the kids,' Jack said. 'Works too hard, mind. But she'll pop in and see us and tell a story to Freddie and Sam or sing to Helena.'

For a mad moment, James found himself hoping that she'd drop in to see her cousins that evening. It'd be good to see her outside the hospital environment—and maybe here she might relax with him.

Nick came out, his shirt splotchy with water. 'Jack, Alison could do with a hand with Freddie and Sam while she puts Helena to bed.'

'Of course.' Jack stood up. 'You remember Dad, don't you, James?'

'I do. Good to see you, Nick,' James said, standing up and shaking his hand. The older man was regarding him coolly. No doubt, James thought, he remembered the fact that he used to party with Jack in London.

'James,' Nick said.

An awkward silence stretched between them as Jack went indoors. James was about to break it when Nick said quietly, 'I overheard you talking about Charlotte. Whatever you're thinking about her, forget it: she's not a challenge for you to conquer.'

Jack had always complained that his father was a control freak. 'With all due respect,' James said, politely but coolly, 'that's between me and Charlotte.'

'Apart from the fact that she's my niece and I don't want to see her hurt,' Nick said, 'she's had a rough time in the last couple of years. She doesn't need any hassles.'

'I'm not going to hassle her.'

'I hope not,' Nick said. 'For her sake.'

On Sunday evening, Nick opened the door and frowned. 'Kate? I wasn't expecting to see you.'

'No.' She paused. 'Can I have a word?'

She looked terrible, Nick thought, as if she hadn't slept for days.

'Sure, come in. Can I get you a coffee or something?'

She shook her head. 'Thanks for the offer, but I don't want anything.'

Now he was starting to get really worried. The last time he'd seen Kate look this drawn had been... No. He didn't want to think about that conversation. 'Come and sit down.' He ushered her through to the living room. 'So what can I do for you?'

She dragged in a breath. 'Nick, I...'

To his horror, he could see her eyes glimmering with tears. Oh, hell. He didn't want her to start crying on him. He couldn't cope with that. Last time she'd cried on his shoulder, it had been a huge mistake. For both of them. They'd let the past get in the way and done something so awful that… Well, they'd both paid the price for it. More than paid.

She scrubbed at her eyes with the back of her hand. 'Sorry, Nick. I'm not going to cry over you.'

Hell and double hell. Surely he hadn't spoken his thoughts aloud? 'What is it, Kate?'

'I…' She wrapped her arms round herself. 'I need to ask you something. Something important.'

This sounded ominous. Unsure what to say, he just nodded.

'Remember the night of the flood? When you promised you'd try, with Jem?'

And he had. He'd even bought Jem a proper Christmas present. Though then that tourist's comment had caught him on the raw and he'd walked away. Now he could acknowledge just how unfair he'd been. Nick raked a hand through his hair. 'I'm not good with kids. I made a mess of things with my own.'

'Jem *is* yours,' Kate said tightly.

Hell. He was digging the hole even deeper. 'I meant, my kids with Annabel.'

She shrugged. 'Things are better between you now.'

'But it's still new. I can't… How are they going to feel if they find out I was unfaithful to their mother?'

'They're adults now. They don't see the world in black and white, the way children do. They understand that sometimes people act in ways you wouldn't normally do.'

And how.

'OK, so you were hard on them,' Kate continued, 'but that's the past. You have to draw a line some time. And you're good with your niece.'

'Charlotte?'

There was a hint of bitterness in her smile. 'Well. You would be. She's the spitting image of Annabel, whereas Jem…' She exhaled sharply. 'Sorry. I didn't come here to have a go at you.'

'Then why did you come, Kate?'

She moistened her lips. 'There isn't an easy way to say this.'

She was getting married to Rob? Well, it was obvious that was the way the wind was blowing. He'd heard the rumours. Everyone in Penhally had. And hadn't he seen it for himself, the night he'd gone over to her house? The two of them, kissing in full view. He'd walked away that night, too.

'I've got cancer.'

As the words sank in, Nick's legs gave way and he sat down heavily. 'Did you just say…?' He found he could hardly say the word. 'Cancer?'

She shivered. 'Yes. Breast cancer. I found a lump.'

It was just like learning of Annabel's death all over again. The shock of hearing something so shocking, so appalling, that he couldn't believe it. He forced himself to ask the question. 'Do you know what stage?' Please don't let it be stage four. Or even stage three. Please don't.

'No. Dr Bower…she thinks it's going to be OK with a lumpectomy. But we won't know for sure until…' Her voice faded.

Until Kate was on the table. Yes. He knew that. 'So when do you go in?'

'Monday next week.'

'Monday next week?' He stared at her in disbelief. 'How long have you known?'

'A few days.'

'A few days, and you didn't say anything?'

'Apart from the fact that you're not my GP, I didn't,' she said with quiet dignity, 'think you'd be that interested.'

'Not be…?' He shook his head, trying to clear it. 'Kate, how have we got to this point?'

She looked suddenly old. 'I'm not here to rake up the past. I thought I'd be OK with this. Thought I'd…'

Nick moved then. Sat next to her on the sofa. Held her close. 'It's OK. And now I know, I can pull some strings and—'

'No.' Kate wriggled out of his arms. 'No need, I've sorted it myself.'

'You always did do things your own way.'

Her eyes glittered. 'What was I supposed to do, Nick? If I'd told you about Jem when I first realised... You were happily married to Annabel. It would've wrecked your marriage and devastated her.'

'And it didn't devastate me, finding out the way I did?'

She wrapped her arms round herself again. 'I knew it was a mistake coming to see you.'

'Then why did you come here, Kate?'

'Because,' she said quietly, 'it's occurred to me. I go under the knife next week. God only knows what Dr Bower will find. With luck, she'll have caught it. But if she hasn't...if I'm not going to make it...there's Jem. I need to know that he's going to be all right.' She shivered again. 'I need to know that you'll take care of him. Be his guardian. Take your place as his father.'

'You want me to—'

'I've thought it through, Nick,' she cut in. 'You and I have known each other for years. Worked with each other for years. Been friends for years.'

Friends? They'd hardly been that recently. And he was still so angry with her about Jem. Angry with himself, and taking it out on her, he acknowledged wryly.

'So nobody's going to bat an eyelid about me asking you to be his guardian. You're the obvious person. And,' she said, holding his gaze steadily, 'like it or not, you're his father. If I don't pull through, he's going to need you.'

Nick swallowed hard. 'I need time to—'

'To think about it?' She shook her head. 'You've had *months* to get used to the idea, Nick. Months to pull your head out of the sand. And now you want more time.'

Her teeth had started to chatter, but when Nick went to put his arms round her again she pulled away. 'The thing is, Nick, I might not *have* time. Yes, we gave in to our emotions. Took comfort from each other on one of the darkest nights of our lives. But it was years ago, we can't change the past, and don't you think we've paid enough for it? And do you really think it's fair to take it out on Jem?'

'Kate, this is all such a—'

'Just forget it, Nick,' she cut in. 'I should've known that you'd let me down.' She stood up. 'I'll see myself out.'

And, before Nick could say another word, she walked out of the house.

On Monday morning, Charlotte was sorting through her list when James walked into her office. 'I would've knocked, but my hands are full,' he said as she glanced up.

Two paper cups of coffee and a paper bag containing something that smelled gorgeous.

'I'll try not to get crumbs on your desk,' he said, setting them all down on her desk and opening the bag. 'But I'm prepared to share, if you like *pain au chocolat*.'

She loved it. Though this felt as if James had somehow commandeered her into having breakfast with him. 'You're being a bit smooth for a Monday morning,' she commented.

'Actually, no. I haven't had breakfast yet and this is about the only time I'm going to get to have it. Also, I know you're a lark and I wanted to talk to you about this morning's list.'

'I see.' She paused. 'Well, thank you for the coffee.' The scent of the warm pastries was too much for her, and she took one. 'And the sugar rush.'

He smiled at her. 'Pleasure.' His voice was almost a purr.

Charlotte swallowed hard, willing her libido to behave. 'So, the list.' Talking to him about work was fine. She could do that. Even smile and laugh with him.

And then he leaned forward. Dabbed the tip of his forefinger on the corner of her mouth—and then licked his finger.

It felt almost as if he'd licked her skin, and her heart skipped a beat. She felt her eyes widen and her lips part, though she couldn't get the question out.

As if he'd realised that she wanted to know why he'd done

it, he said softly, 'You had chocolate on the corner of your mouth.'

Oh-h-h.

'I just about stopped myself doing what I really wanted to do,' he said, his voice growing husky.

And this time—when she wanted the words to stay back—they spilled out involuntarily. 'What was that?'

Time seemed to stretch. And then he leaned forward and kissed the corner of her mouth, just where his fingertip had touched her moments before.

If anyone else had tried that, she would've pushed them away.

But with James…she was shocked by how much she wanted to turn her head slightly, allow his mouth closer contact with hers. How much she wanted to slide her fingers into his hair and kiss him back.

She pulled away and dragged in a breath. 'That…'

'Wasn't very professional of me and it shouldn't have happened,' James said.

And then, instead of the 'I'm sorry' she was half expecting, he added, 'Not at work.'

This was her cue to tell him it wasn't going to happen out of work either. Except her mouth was refusing to be sensible and say it.

She was sure he guessed at the turmoil going on in her head, because he said softly, 'I'd better let you get on with your paperwork.'

'Uh-huh.'

But even after he left her office, she couldn't stop thinking about him. Couldn't stop remembering how his mouth had felt against hers. A brief caress, cherishing rather than commanding.

Not like Michael.

But she was trembling. She dragged in a breath, and went through the grounding technique she'd learned and was teaching others—she sat down, held the arms of her chair and set her feet flat on the floor to make herself feel grounded. And then she focused on naming five things she could see. 'Desk, chair, door, window, computer.' Five things to hear, five things she could touch, five scents, five tastes… She went through each in turn, took a deep breath, and finally she felt still and calm inside.

Just as long as she didn't think about James.

On Tuesday, James dropped in casually to Charlotte's office. Considering that even her cousin had said she was too serious, it was time for Charlotte to realise that it was OK to have fun.

Preferably with him.

Which meant she needed to get used to him being around.

Then he noticed the framed photograph on her desk. 'Is that your cat?'

She nodded. 'Pandora.'

The name he'd puzzled over before…and it turned out that Pandora was a *cat*. He was careful not to let the relief show on his face. 'Nice cat,' he commented. 'What sort is she?'

'A Burmese blue.'

'How long have you had her?'

'Since a couple of weeks after I came to Cornwall.'

He smiled. 'You're determined not to talk to me, aren't you?'

'Don't be ridiculous.'

'You're going to have to talk to me a lot more, you know. When your team loses tonight and you have dinner with me.'

'My team isn't going to lose.'

He laughed. 'Tell me that later tonight.' He blew her a kiss. 'Catch you later.'

Charlotte set the cookies she'd made earlier on the table with the other refreshments. She always enjoyed these evenings, but tonight she was nervous. Because of that stupid bet. She'd better hope that James had a weak spot, because she couldn't back out of it now. And if he won...

She joined her team at the table and tried to chat normally with Steffie and Tim and the others, but she knew the very second that James walked in the door. She couldn't help turning round, and he looked utterly stunning. It was the first time she'd seen him in casual clothes—OK, they were clearly designer jeans and probably cost more than her entire outfit put together, but the faded denims suited him. They clung in all the right places. He'd teamed it with a white shirt, but it was casual rather than the formal ones he wore at work, with an open neck and sleeves rolled up to his elbows. He looked utterly gorgeous, very touchable, and the question slipped insidiously into her head: was James the man who could make her forget the past?

The first three rounds of the quiz were all fairly close, and then it started getting serious. And somehow Charlotte had ended up sitting in a position where she could see James's face. His expression told her that he was playing to win.

Charlotte looked utterly gorgeous in jeans, scoop-necked pastel pink T-shirt and just a hint of lipstick. James was pretty sure she'd changed and got ready in less than five minutes—unlike his previous girlfriends and Sophia, who'd taken almost two hours to get ready, with immaculately coiffed hair and flawless full make-up. With her hair loose, Charlotte looked like the girl next door and he'd just bet she didn't have a clue about just how beautiful she was.

In the first couple of rounds, when she'd been laughing with her team, she'd looked relatively carefree, but he noticed in the break that she looked slightly tense. Because of him?

Maybe he could tease her out of it. 'We're neck and neck, Miss Moneypenny.'

'Don't count your chickens, Bond. There are still five rounds to go.'

Dave from the emergency department came over. 'You

know, Charlotte, considering you come down to our place so often to work with us, I reckon you ought to be on our team.'

'Not a chance! She's ours,' Tim declared, draping his arm round her shoulders. 'Hands off.'

Jealousy flickered through James, shocking him. For pity's sake, he knew that Tim was married and Charlotte saw him simply as her colleague. But at the same time he noticed that she was so much more relaxed with Dave and Tim than she was with him—and it rankled.

'I want more cake,' Charlotte said, gently disengaging herself from Tim's hug.

'Ah, now I know the way to you is through your stomach, I'll learn how to make fabulous cakes—and I'll woo you over to my team,' Dave teased.

'In your dreams, Davey-boy,' Charlotte said with a grin.

She'd clearly worked with both of them for a long time and got on well with them, James thought, but she wouldn't let either of them put their arms around her for long. So maybe it *wasn't* just him.

'Are you enjoying yourself, James?' Lisa asked. 'I know it's probably a far cry from the kind of fundraisers you're used to—we have the Christmas ball, but that's the only really big one.'

'It all adds up, and the important thing about fundraising is to have fun,' James said.

'Oh, I'm all for fun,' Lisa said with a bright smile, flicking her hair back. 'I was wondering…seeing as you're fairly new around here, maybe you'd like me to show you around a bit. Show you where the night life is in St Piran.'

'That's really kind of you to ask me,' he said, smiling at her, 'but, as you say, I'm still finding my feet a bit. I'm not really ready to start seeing anyone.' It wasn't strictly true. If Charlotte had made the same offer, he'd have taken it up in a nanosecond—but he didn't see the point in being rude and hurting the younger doctor.

It was still neck and neck between the cardio team and the

surgeons when the last round started. And James smiled to himself at the last question: the location of a really obscure island.

He knew exactly where it was.

His father owned it.

And, given the level of muttering around the room, nobody else had a clue where it was.

Which meant that his team was going to win.

Then he remembered what Nick had said. *She's not a challenge for you to conquer... She's had a rough time in the last couple of years.*

He glanced over at her at almost exactly the moment she glanced at him.

And the worry in her eyes decided him. He'd fib and say he didn't know the answer; the teams would tie, and the bet would be off. Along with all the pressure.

'Don't have a clue,' he said blandly.

But when the answers were read out, he discovered that he'd miscalculated.

It wasn't a draw.

Charlotte's team had won.

There was something fishy about this, Charlotte thought. Although James had looked surprised when her team had won, she'd seen the expression on his face at the last question. He'd known the answer. And yet his team had got the question wrong.

Had he deliberately let her win?

She drew a slip of paper from the old chocolate tin. 'The money goes to the Friends of the Hospital for their Christmas fund.'

'That's brilliant.' Dave took the envelope. 'I'll drop the money in to them tomorrow before I go on duty.'

She said her goodbyes, then hurried after James and laid her hand on his arm. The feel of his bare skin against hers sent a shiver down her spine. 'James, have you got a moment?'

'Of course,' he said politely.

She didn't want this discussion in front of everyone. 'Maybe I can walk you to your car?'

'I came by bike.'

She blinked. 'Motorbike?' She could just imagine him as a bad boy in black leathers. Like the picture of the Australian actor that Steffie kept on the pinboard behind her desk. Shockingly, it made her knees feel weak.

'Pushbike,' James corrected.

'Right.' She walked with him over to the bike shelter. Once she was sure there wasn't an audience, she said softly, 'That last question—you knew the answer.'

'I thought I did. Obviously I got it wrong.'

She shook her head. 'Don't lie to me, James. You deliberately got it wrong so you wouldn't beat me. Why?'

'Honestly?'

She nodded. 'Honestly.'

'That bet I made with you. It wasn't fair. I was bullying you and I was wrong—and, actually, I thought we were level pegging so I threw the question to make us even.'

'Making all bets off.'

He nodded.

'I still don't understand why.'

'I've been involved with someone who didn't want to be involved with me. I'm not going to make that mistake again.'

There was nothing she could say to that without prying. She spread her hands helplessly. 'Thank you.'

'You won,' he said. 'And I made a deal with you. So I'll leave you alone.'

'You miscalculated, and you meant to do the right thing,' she said. 'So I think we'll stick with your original intention. All bets off.'

'A new deal.'

His gaze flickered from her mouth to her eyes and back again. And again. And when she didn't pull away, he bent his head. Brushed his lips very, very gently against hers.

It was like fireworks going off in her head. Fireworks that really shouldn't be there. She wasn't in the market for a relationship, and she wasn't the kind of glamorous woman James normally dated.

And yet...

One more kiss, so sweet and soft and fleeting that she wondered if she'd dreamed it.

'Thank you,' he said. 'That's sealed it. Friends?'

Friends didn't kiss each other like that. Friends didn't look at each other like that.

'Friends,' she said shakily.

'Would I be pushing my luck if I offered to walk you home?'

'James, I'm twenty-eight.'

He smiled wryly. 'You're a grown woman and you can look after yourself. Message received and understood.' He unlocked his bike. 'See you tomorrow.'

When Charlotte got home, she sat on the sofa with her cat draped over her and purring away. What James had said about being involved with someone who didn't want to be involved with him... She had a feeling he was talking about his ex-wife. The paparazzi had shown him as partying away regardless of their marriage breakdown, but maybe that had been as much of a false front as the one she'd learned to put up, something to hide how hurt he really was.

Maybe, just maybe, he wasn't who she'd thought he was.

CHAPTER SEVEN

THE following morning, James walked onto the cardiology ward.

'Here's our hotshot surgeon,' Steffie teased. 'I thought you said you were going to make us eat crow?' She made the shape of an L on her forehead and laughed. 'Actually, it was pretty close. You gave us a real run for our money—everyone's still buzzing about what a good night it was.'

He wondered if that included Charlotte. 'I enjoyed it, too. And was that lemon cake yours?'

'Yes.'

'If you weren't already married,' he said with a grin, 'I'd think about asking you. Just so I could have cake like that every single day.'

Steffie flapped a dismissive hand. 'Yeah, yeah.'

He smiled. 'By the way, is your team captain around? I wanted a quick word with her about Brianna on my list.'

'Sorry, she's not in today.'

'She's off duty?' Though she hadn't said a word to him about it yesterday.

'Actually, she's off every Wednesday from now on.'

Surprise turned to worry. 'Steffie, I hope I'm not asking out of turn—but is everything all right?'

'It's fine. She's just negotiated different working hours—she spreads her time over four days a week at the hospital instead of five, and on Wednesdays she's working in Penhally, just down the road.'

He knew Penhally. The seaside village where Jack lived. 'What's she doing in Penhally?'

'Her uncle's the senior partner in the GP practice there.'

He knew Nick, too.

'She's doing some sessions at the women's clinic.'

'The women's clinic? Not what I'd expect from a cardiologist.' Strange: it was out of her specialty. Then the penny dropped. 'Of course. With obesity and diabetes on the rise, it makes sense to talk to people about heart health, and drop-in sessions at a GP clinic is a good way to do it—if she's doing the women's clinic, she must be talking to the women on the surgery's obesity register, the diabetics and the postmenopausal women.'

'That's what she thought—she says that preventive medicine is the way forward to relieve pressure on us.'

'Great idea.'

'And then there's her rape crisis centre.'

'Rape crisis centre?' James echoed. Hmm. For Charlotte to change her hours at the hospital so she could work a day a week pro bono…that had to be personal.

'She's a bit cagey on the subject,' Steffie said, 'but I think it happened to someone close to her, a while before she moved to Cornwall. This is her way of doing something to help. Putting something back. That's Charlotte all over.'

He'd met plenty of doctors who'd chosen their specialty because of something personal to them; it was the obvious reason why someone would choose to do something outside their own speciality.

But then something else clicked. Nick had said that Charlotte had been through a rough time. He could've meant that she'd supported a friend through an ordeal and had found it draining; but he could also have meant that Charlotte herself had gone through the ordeal.

And that would explain why Charlotte had gone to the lengths of negotiating different hours at the hospital.

So maybe it hadn't happened to someone close to her. Maybe it had happened to Charlotte herself—not that he could possibly ask her. But it would explain a lot.

And he needed to show her that she could trust him, as well as have fun with him.

On Thursday lunchtime, James was delighted when Charlotte knocked on his office door. She felt comfortable enough to meet him on his territory, then?

'James, I know you have a lecture this afternoon at the university rather than a stint in Theatre, but can I have a really quick word about one of my patients?'

'Sure. Come and sit down.'

'It's Ellis Martyn.'

He flicked through his memory. 'The boy with Ebstein's—you've got his portable recorder readings back?'

'Yep—and I'm not happy.'

He nodded. 'Put me in the picture.'

'He's coming up for thirteen, just finished his first year in high school. He's been complaining of his heart racing and "hiccuping"—he's tired a lot of the time, he's short of breath and he's been having a hard time in PE lessons. His mum says he's just started being a bit blue round the lips, and the GP referred him to me. The X-ray showed his heart's enlarged, the echo showed his tricuspid valve is leaking, and the portable recorder showed episodes of tachycardia.'

'So you're thinking extra pathways?'

'Yes. I can sort that out with ablation, but I'm going to need you to sort the valve.'

'Are the echo and ECG images on the system?' he asked.

'Yes.'

He logged in to the system and pulled them up. 'Mmm, the

right atrium is really enlarged, and I can see here the tricuspid valve needs repair. When are you seeing him next?'

'Tomorrow morning.'

'OK. Let me know what time, and I'll come and talk to him and his parents.'

'Just his mum, Judy,' she said. 'His dad works in London during the week.'

'Ouch. That's tough on her.'

To Charlotte's relief, James was as good as his word and came in to see the Martyns the next morning.

'Thanks for dropping off the recorder yesterday,' Charlotte said to Judy. 'It's picked up several of the episodes where your heart was beating too fast, Ellis, and I've asked Mr Alexander to join us this morning—he's our specialist cardiac surgeon.'

'So Ellis needs surgery?' Judy asked.

'We both think so, yes.' She introduced James swiftly to them—and noticed that he had his James Bond watch on again. But instead of looking excited, the way Danny had, Ellis looked wary.

'Surgeons have this bad habit of needing flashy stuff,' she said to Ellis with a smile, 'but I happen to know that this one works very hard and is really good at his job. So ignore anything he says about being like James Bond.'

'Busted,' James said with a smile. 'Ellis, there's a valve in your heart called the tricuspid valve—it's called that because it has three flaps, pretty much the same way a triceratops got its name—'

'Because it has three horns,' Ellis chipped in.

'Spot on.' James smiled at the boy. 'In your case, two of the flaps are stuck to the wall of the heart, where they shouldn't be, so the valve can't do its job properly.'

'Charlotte told me it leaked when it shouldn't, so the deoxy-genated blood goes into my body instead of into my lungs,' Ellis continued.

James was pretty sure that Charlotte had explained it in

simpler terms, but clearly the boy was comfortable with scientific terms and had probably looked up his condition on the Internet. 'It's good that you know all that—it saves me banging on and repeating it all for you. Though I also know it's a lot to take in, so Charlotte and I are both more than happy to answer any questions you might have.'

'Is there no alternative to surgery?' Judy asked.

'I know it's worrying for you,' James said gently, 'and, yes, I'll be frank with you, there are always risks with surgery under a general anaesthetic. But if you leave it he's going to need surgery in the future and he might need a complete heart transplant, whereas now I can repair the tricuspid valve and it's not such a huge operation to get over. It's also better to do it when he's younger than to leave it until he's an adult—there are less likely to be any complications in surgery.'

'So when do I have to have it done?' Ellis asked.

'I have a slot free Monday morning,' James said.

'Monday? That quickly?' Judy looked shocked. 'But I thought people had to wait months for an operation?' She clapped her hand to her mouth in horror. 'Does this mean it's really serious?'

James, seeing the anguish in the woman's face said, 'All it means is that I have a slot free on Monday morning. I was lecturing, but my session has been moved, and because I knew I was going to see you with Charlotte this morning I've already checked out the bed and Theatre situation. We're in luck, so that's why it's free.'

'Ellis's condition is serious and it's rare,' Charlotte added, 'but it's also fixable and he'll go on to live a perfectly normal life.'

'Monday,' Ellis said.

'You don't have to decide right now,' James said. 'Take your time. But it's good timing for you because it means you'll have most of the summer holidays to recover from the operation and get fit for school again ready for the new term, though you might miss the first week or so. The good news is that it will make a huge difference to you—you won't feel tired all the time and you won't get breathless in PE.'

'I hate PE,' Ellis said.

'It'll be a lot easier for you when you're heart's working properly,' James reassured him. 'You might find it's not so bad then.'

'Will the operation stop my heart racing?' Ellis asked.

'No, because that's not caused by the valve,' Charlotte said. 'It's all because of some extra electrical pathways in your heart—they give an extra impulse to make your heart beat when it shouldn't. Don't worry, it's really common and we can sort it out during surgery—or if you decide you don't want to have surgery yet, I can sort that out for you in our cath lab as a day patient. You'll be able to go home the same day I've done it.'

'So how does the cath lab work?' Judy asked.

'What I'll do is put a special probe to Ellis's heart to where the extra pathways are, and then send a radio signal down to stop the pathways sending the signals.' She smiled at Ellis. 'It's very similar to the way microwave heat works, so you can gross out all your mates by telling them I'm going to microwave your heart.'

Ellis brightened at that, and then looked worried. 'Will it hurt?'

'No, because I'll give you a special local anaesthetic called sedation. It won't hurt, but you might be a little bit uncomfortable afterwards. The sedation means you won't remember much of what I do, but your mum can stay with you if she likes.'

'Microwave and sliced,' Ellis said thoughtfully.

James smiled. 'Or I can just do the slicing and sort out the pathways for you at the same time.'

'You're not going to microwave me?'

'Nope. They used to do it by surgery, but there's an even better way now—something called cryoablation.' He deliberately used the technical term, knowing that the boy would like it—if necessary, he'd explain it in layman's terms, but his guess was that Ellis would work it out.

'Cryo…' Ellis thought for a moment. 'What, freezing?'

'Exactly.'

'So I'll be freezed and sliced.' Ellis looked at his mother. 'I think I've just decided to become a vegetarian.'

Judy ruffled his hair. 'Whatever you want, love. It's up to you.'

'If I don't have surgery, I'm still going to be ill.' He took a deep breath. 'Will I have to come back to hospital a lot afterwards?'

'You'll be able to live a completely normal life,' James said.

'Though you will come back for regular check-ups,' Charlotte added, 'and you'll be able to ring me any time you're worried.'

'Can we have some time to think about it?' Judy asked.

'As much time as you need,' James said. 'I can give you a leaflet about the procedure if that'll help you, and you can come back and ask me questions when you've had a chance to read it.'

'Thank you,' Judy said.

'May I?' He gestured to the computer next to Charlotte.

'Sure.'

He logged her out, tapped in his password, scrolled quickly through some files and then printed off a leaflet and gave it to the Martyns. 'That should tell you everything to expect, but I know you'll have questions and I'm more than happy to answer them, when you're ready.'

'Go and have a walk or something to eat,' Charlotte said. 'The café here is good. Come back and see us…' She looked at James for an idea of timing.

'I'll be at the hospital for the next hour,' James said, 'but then I'll be lecturing until the middle of the afternoon. But if not now, we can talk on Monday. The operation doesn't have to be

Monday morning—we can schedule it later, if that's better for you.'

'Thank you,' Ellis said.

'I appreciate this,' Charlotte said when the Martyns had left.

'No problem. That's what teamwork's all about,' James said softly.

'Teamwork.'

'We're a good team.' He paused. 'And I think we'd make a good team outside work.'

'We agreed that we'll be friends.'

'Absolutely.' He looked her straight in the eye. 'But I didn't say anything about excluding any other kind of relationship. And, actually, I'd rather date someone I happen to like and trust and respect.'

'Like and trust and respect,' she echoed, looking dazed.

He leaned forward so he could whisper in her ear. 'As well as fancying the pants off.' He pressed a kiss to the sensitive spot behind her ear, then left her office before she could gather her wits enough to make a smart retort.

And he was faintly disappointed that when he got back after his lecture there was a brief and very professional email from her in his inbox, telling her that the Martyns had decided in favour of the operation.

She was clearly avoiding him.

Running scared.

Maybe he should take it just a little slower. Maybe. But he certainly wasn't going to give up.

On Saturday afternoon, Charlotte was sitting drinking coffee at Nick's house, chatting, when James's name came up.

'Is he bothering you?' Nick asked. 'If he is, I'll have another word with him.'

'Another?' She was horrified that Nick had had a word with him already. Especially as James hadn't mentioned it to her.

'Or I'll get Jack to do it, if you'd rather,' Nick offered.

'No, it's fine. Nick, I know you mean well, and it's lovely that you're being so protective, but…' She sighed. 'I'm not going to be rude and tell you not to interfere. Thank you for thinking of me, but I can handle this myself—really, I can.'

Nick gave her an appraising look. 'So you like him?'

She really wasn't prepared to talk about her feelings for James yet. She still needed to sort them out in her head. 'I'm happy as I am. I love my work and don't want that to change. And even if I was interested in James, which I'm not.' Ha, who was she trying to kid? She couldn't stop thinking about him. 'I'm not sure I could handle all the celebrity stuff that goes with him.' She'd hated the idea of her photograph being in the press and people gossiping about her; she'd been seriously relieved when the picture from the pub hadn't turned up anywhere.

'Why don't you have a word with Melinda?' Nick suggested.

Charlotte remembered all the headlines, the previous year, when Melinda had been outed as the future ruler of Contarini; the press had absolutely hounded her. It was all much quieter now and Melinda was plain Mrs Lovak, the local vet, but she was sure that Melinda didn't want to be reminded of all that stuff again. 'It's not fair to intrude like that.'

'Trust me, Dragan used to be even more wary of people than you are, before Melinda came along—and if you want an excuse to talk to her, you can always go and tell her how Pandora's doing. You know she loves hearing how her rescue cases are getting on. And their dog's expecting puppies, so she might try and talk you into giving one a good home.'

'Puppies…I'll bear that in mind.' Charlotte looked at her uncle. There were deep shadows beneath his eyes. 'Nick, it's my turn to interfere now. You look as if you haven't slept properly for a couple of weeks.'

He flapped a dismissive hand. 'It's the surgery. Dragan's cut his hours, Adam and Maggie are leaving at the end of next month, and even though we've got Polly on board now, it's still not enough to cover all the work.'

Charlotte raised an eyebrow. 'Nick, that's not the sort of thing you worry about. You just sort things. Annabel always said you were really good at organising things. It's more than that, isn't it?'

Nick's face tightened. 'I don't want to discuss it. Look, I need to be somewhere. Go and see Melinda about the pups.'

Charlotte, knowing that once her uncle had clammed up it was impossible to get him to talk, gave in. She kissed him lightly on the cheek. 'Well, thanks for the coffee. Try and get some sleep, and stop overdoing it.'

Nick made no comment.

'And, Nick?' When he looked up, Charlotte added softly, 'You were there for me when I needed you. So I hope you know that it's the same for you. If you do decide you want to talk, I'll listen without judging, and I won't go and blab to anyone else.'

For a moment, she thought she saw tears in her uncle's eyes, but it must have been a trick of the light. Nick never cried. 'Thanks,' he said gruffly.

He wasn't going to tell her any more, she knew, so she headed off to see Melinda and Dragan.

'Charlotte!' Melinda greeted her warmly. 'Lovely to see you, *cara*. We're in the back garden. Come through. How's Pandora?'

'She's doing fine.' Charlotte showed Melinda the latest pictures on her mobile phone.

'Pwetty tat,' Alessandro announced, climbing onto Charlotte's lap and peering at the screen before wriggling down again and joining the flatcoat retriever in the paddling pool.

'I'm really not sure Bramble should be in the pool,' Dragan said, looking concerned.

Melinda rolled her eyes. 'Stop fussing, *zlato*. Honestly, Charlotte, he's nearly as bad as he was when I was expecting

Alessandro. Dragan, Bramble will be fine. A flattie's idea of heaven is a paddling pool and a tennis ball, and someone who doesn't mind getting wet too.'

Little Alessandro, who was the image of his father, except he had Melinda's golden hair and curls.

'I know that, and I wouldn't mind, but—'

'She's expecting her first litter next month,' Melinda said.

'Nick told me—and also that you were looking for good homes.'

'Ah, so you're offering one. *Bene*.' Melinda laughed. 'You can guarantee Dragan's going to want to be there through every step and he'll be *terrible* when she has the pups.'

'There's nothing wrong with the fact that I love my dog and I worry about her,' Dragan protested. 'It's a big thing, having babies.'

'I'm going to have to switch my phone off when she starts labour, or you'll be calling me every ten minutes, just as you did when I was close to having Alessandro.'

'Every ten minutes,' Dragan said thoughtfully. 'Between patients. Mmm, sounds about right.'

'Dragan Lovak, you're impossible.' Melinda smiled. 'But I love you.'

He kissed her lightly. '*Volim te.* I love you, too.'

Charlotte saw the tenderness in his face. He was clearly so much in love with his wife. And the way he looked at her...It was how she'd once wanted someone to look at her.

Funny how James's face was so clear in her mind's eye.

Dragan's phone beeped; he answered the call, then moved away slightly before ending it and coming back over to them. 'I'm needed. Sorry, *carissima*,' he said to Melinda.

'Hey, I knew you were on call today. It's not a problem.'

He kissed her and Alessandro goodbye, and shook Charlotte's hand. 'See you at the surgery on Wednesday, if you're not here when I get back.'

'Sure.'

When Dragan had gone, Melinda made them all a cold drink. 'All right, now you can tell me what's really wrong.'

'Nothing's wrong,' Charlotte said.

Melinda raised an eyebrow. 'It's lovely to see how Pandora's doing, but that isn't why you came, is it?'

Charlotte sighed. 'It's a bit awkward.'

'Tell me anyway.'

Charlotte bit her lip. 'I apologise in advance...but you're the only one I know who's had to deal with the press.'

'You're having problems with the press?'

'Um...sort of. Someone I know who gets followed by the press. We were having dinner together, just as friends, and we were photographed. It didn't bother him.'

'But it bothered you?'

Charlotte nodded.

'You do get used to it,' Melinda said. 'And dealing with press isn't so bad. You just keep saying "No comment", and scope places out in advance so you know the back way out.'

Just how James had dealt with it—sneaking her out to the taxi driver. 'And it's that easy?'

'Well...not easy, perhaps,' Melinda admitted. 'When the story broke about us, Dragan found the paparazzi thing hard. But if he's worth it you'll find a way round it.'

'That's the point. I didn't intend to date anyone.'

'But he's different?' Melinda guessed.

'I can't get him out of my head,' Charlotte confessed. 'Even when I try private visualisation techniques, he's suddenly there with me—it's meant to be just me on this deserted beach, and suddenly he's there, holding my hand.'

'Maybe you need to give him a chance, *cara*.' Melinda gave her a hug. 'I know you don't talk about things—just like my Dragan—but sometimes it can help.'

'Maybe.' Charlotte gave her a wry smile. 'I really ought to be going.'

'Come back and see the puppies.'

'I will.'

'And maybe bring your man with you. How he is with children and animals…that's a good way to tell someone's character.'

'He's brilliant with kids, actually—he charms them, but doesn't talk down to them.'

'Then I'd say half your battle's won. Does he like animals?'

Charlotte spread her hands. 'I have no idea.'

'There's only one way to find out,' Melinda said sagely.

On Saturday evening, when the boys were still playing in the garden, Rob curled up with Kate on the sofa. 'I was thinking,' Rob said. 'I'd like you to come and stay with us when you're out of hospital. It means you can rest whenever you need to and not worry about Jem, because he'll be with me and Matt, and I'll be happier because I'll know you're not overdoing it.'

Kate shivered. If only Nick had responded to her like this. If only Nick had been the kind of man she could lean on. She'd loved him for so many years, and yet he'd let her down time and time again. Whereas Rob was a man with a big heart, a man who cared about her and about Jem, in a way Nick never could.

She knew she was lucky to have him. He was good for her, and she intended to be good for him, too. Unable to speak, she just held him tightly.

Rob stroked her hair. 'Of course you're worried. You wouldn't be human if you weren't. But you know what the doctor said. I was with you. The chances are, they've caught it early enough.'

'I know.' She swallowed hard. 'And it's a hell of a choice to make, Rob. Lose my breast and know there wasn't any tissue left for the cancer to get into, but also not be able to use my arm properly for months and months; or have the lumpectomy so it'll be less of a problem, but I'll need radiotherapy every day for five weeks, which is going to make me knackered.'

'Damned if you do, damned if you don't.' He brushed a kiss

against her mouth. 'Whatever happens, Kate, I'll be there for you. And, just for the record, if you do have a mastectomy, you won't be any less of a woman to me.'

The backs of Kate's eyelids pricked with tears. It had been one of the things running through her head. How she'd feel less of a woman. How she wouldn't be able to wear pretty, low-cut tops any more—and even after reconstructive surgery she'd be wary of anyone seeing her body again.

'I love you, Kate Althorp. And you'll always be beautiful to me,' Rob said softly.

Kate couldn't speak for the tears clogging her throat.

'And if you need radiotherapy, remember it's the school holidays, so I've got time off. I can drive you to St Piran's for the treatment, and the boys and I will have some serious competitions on their games consoles while we're waiting for you. And then you can rest when we get home, while I take them out to burn off some steam.'

'Oh, Rob. I can't ask you to do that much for me.'

'You're not asking,' he said simply. 'I'm offering.'

An offer that Jem's father hadn't made. An offer that Jem's father hadn't even *considered* making. Total support.

'I like Jem,' Rob continued. 'He's a good kid, he's a good friend to my Matthew, and Matt and I both like having him around.'

A tear leaked out before she could blink it back. Rob wiped it away tenderly with the pad of his thumb. 'You're not alone, Kate. You've got Jem, you've got me and you've got Matt. And we'll get through this.'

'What if…?' she whispered.

'It won't come to that,' Rob said firmly. 'But, if it does, Jem will always have a home with me. And I'll tell him every day what a wonderful woman his mother is.'

She swallowed hard. 'I don't deserve you.'

'Yes, you do.'

'And, Rob…it's lovely of you to offer me somewhere to stay,

but—I feel terrible saying this, when you've been so good to me. It's just…I'd rather go back to my own home, have my own things around me.'

'Of course you would. I wasn't thinking.' He smiled at her. 'Then how about Matt and I come and stay with you? Same deal, just your place instead of mine.'

Rob was prepared to move in with her? 'The cottage only has two bedrooms.'

He stroked her face. 'Matt can use a sleeping bag and camp out in Jem's room, or if the weather's good they can have a tent in the back garden—they'll love it. And I'm not going to push myself on you, love. I'll sleep on the sofa or use a sleeping bag myself.'

She rested against him. 'Sorry, Rob, I'm making a fuss over nothing. Of course you don't have to sleep on the sofa. My bed's big enough.'

'I know I'm being pushy, but I want to be there for you, Kate. Because I love you.'

'I love you, too,' Kate said, and hated herself for the insidious thought that she didn't love him with the same grand passion she'd once had for Nick.

But she was older now.

Wiser.

With Rob, she'd have a love that would last. The kind of love she'd never be able to have with Nick, because he just wasn't capable of it.

To say yes to him now would be the best thing she could do—for all of them. 'Thank you, Rob.'

'So that's a yes?'

She nodded. 'That's a yes.'

CHAPTER EIGHT

ON MONDAY, Charlotte agreed to sit in on Ellis's operation. And it was a real revelation to her: she was impressed by the way James worked—his organisation and the deftness of his hands. She couldn't help thinking of those hands holding hers. Touching her. Coaxing a response from her. Turning her to flame.

He would be gentle with her, she knew; he couldn't do such intricate work if he wasn't gentle. And the way he'd touched her, kissed her so far, he'd been gentle. He wouldn't push her too far, too fast.

She couldn't resist teasing him a tiny bit afterwards. 'So you dress like everyone else, then? I'm surprised you haven't had some designer scrubs made.'

'What, with pictures of Mars all over it, to match my ego?' he shot back.

She grinned. 'Or should we make that Jupiter after all?'

'Very funny.' He frowned. 'I'm not that flashy.'

'Yes, you are. Do you possess any clothes that aren't designer?'

When he didn't answer, she said, 'QED. That proves my case, I think.'

He sighed. 'Look, it's how I was brought up. With a mum who was a supermodel and a dad who owns an international leisure business, what do you expect?'

She winced. 'Sorry, James.' And it was a genuine apology. 'I really didn't mean to stamp on a sore spot.'

'It's not that sore—but if you feel guilty, that's good. You can always buy me a coffee to make up for it, after we've seen Judy and told her the good news.'

'Black, no sugar, right?'

James was pleased that she remembered. And even more pleased when, after they'd seen Judy, she suggested they make it lunch rather than coffee.

'So how's the cat—Pandora, yes?'

'She's fine.' To James's pleasure, Charlotte actually opened up to him. 'Pandora used to belong to an old lady in the out-skirts of Penhally. The neighbours were worried one day when they saw milk bottles on the doorstep and couldn't get an answer from her. They thought she might have been taken ill, and they couldn't get hold of her daughter to get the spare key, so they broke the door down. It terrified Pandora; when she ran outside, they chased her and shouted because they were scared that she'd run into the road and be hit by a car, but all the noise frightened her even more and she ran away.'

'Poor cat,' James said.

'Eventually, she came back and the neighbours took her to Melinda, the vet in Penhally, knowing she'd find the cat a tem-porary home.' She wrinkled her nose. 'Melinda looked after Pandora herself, as she thought it would only be couple of days until Mrs Parker came out of hospital. But sadly Mrs Parker died. I was on duty at the time and had to get in touch with her GP, Dragan Lovak. I didn't realise it, but he was seeing Melinda and obviously he put her in the picture. It must've come up at practice meeting, too, because Nick knew I used to have a Burmese blue when I was little. He rang me and asked if I would take her on.'

'And you did.'

She nodded. 'Pandora's still a bit nervous of men, espe-cially if they have a loud voice, but she's settled in pretty well with me.' She looked at him. 'How about you? Did you ever have a cat?'

'I've never really had that much to do with animals,' he said. 'I always wanted a dog when I was a kid, but because Mum was always jetting off on photo-shoots and Dad was busy with his hotel chain, I went to boarding school. I used to talk my housemaster into letting me walk his dog and pretended she was mine.' He was surprised to find himself telling her things he'd never told anyone, even Sophia. But, then, there was something about Charlotte that made him feel it was safe to talk—that she wouldn't laugh at him if he told her something important to him, and she wouldn't tell anyone else either.

'Every Christmas I used to write my letter to Santa and ask for a black puppy with a shiny nose called Dylan, who'd sleep on my bed and be my best friend,' he said wistfully. 'Of course, it never happened. But maybe one day. When I'm settled.' And the way things were going, he was beginning to think that Jack Tremayne had made the right choice. This little corner of Cornwall was the perfect place to settle.

At the end of lunch, he said softly, 'Thank you.'

Charlotte looked surprised. 'What for?'

'Giving me a chance.'

'I enjoyed it, too,' she said.

'Maybe we can do this again some time.'

'I'd like that.'

He knew he was probably pushing it, but he asked anyway. 'How about tomorrow?'

She paused, as if weighing it up, and then she nodded. 'Tomorrow.'

'Great.' He scanned the corridor quickly. Deserted. Perfect. He leaned forward, cupped her face with one hand and kissed her lightly. He half expected her to take a step back, and then she really surprised him, by resting her fingers against his cheek and kissing him back.

A tiny kiss.

Nothing that would warrant catcalls from a passing colleague.

But it made James wanted to punch the air and yell in
triumph.

He didn't, not wanting to lose the ground he'd already
gained. Instead, he made a huge effort to sound calm and
serene. 'Tomorrow. I'll look forward to it.'

Kate opened her eyes, feeling as if she'd just gone ten rounds
with a boxer. Dr Bower was sitting next to her, checking a
chart. 'Hello,' she said with a smile. 'Good to see you're back
with us.'

'How did it go?' Kate croaked.

'I've done a wide excision. I'm pretty sure we've got it all
and the radiotherapy will sort out anything that's thinking about
lurking. Obviously I'll know more in a few days, but in the
meantime try not to worry.'

Kate lay back against the bed and closed her eyes. Her over-
whelming thought was that she still had a long way to go, but
she was on the right road now. *She would be there to see Jem
grow up.* She could feel hot tears of relief leaking out. 'Thank
you,' she whispered.

'I'm going to stay here with you for a few more minutes until
you're properly awake, and then your family can see you.
They've been waiting outside, looking pretty anxious. I'll go
and tell them you're awake.' Dr Bower smiled at her again. 'And
I'll let you tell them the good news.'

Over the next couple of days, Kate had plenty of visitors. Polly
dropped in every day, and Rob brought Jem and Matt to see her.

'Rob took us out on the bikes and to the beach—Mum, wait
till you're better and we'll take you,' Jem said excitedly.

Kate summoned a smile despite her tiredness. 'I'd like that,
love.'

'And you'll be home in a couple of days. I can't wait! Rob's going to put up a tent in our back garden so me and Matt can camp out. He's going to teach us how to make a proper camp fire and everything. It's going to be so cool—just we're not going to eat bugs like the celebrities do in the jungle, we're going to cook sausages and burgers,' Jem informed her.

Kate couldn't help laughing.

But then suddenly everyone went quiet and she looked up to see Nick at the foot of her bed, with a huge bunch of flowers.

And there was a distinctly territorial glance between the two men.

'Uncle Nick.' Jem regarded him warily.

'Hello, Jem.' Nick gave him a tight smile, and nodded to the others. 'Rob. Matthew.'

Rob looked at Kate, clearly wanting to know if she'd prefer him to stay or go. She gave him the tiniest nod, to let him know that she was fine and she could deal with this.

'Come on, guys. Let's go and get a drink and give Kate a bit of a break,' Rob said, standing up ready to shepherd the boys out of Kate's cubicle.

'No, it's all right. I won't stay long,' Nick said. 'I just brought you these from the practice, Kate.'

Oh. So the flowers weren't just from him, then. Kate's breathing stilled for a moment. Surely Nick, knowing that Polly was visiting every day, would've sent them in with her to save himself the trip to St Piran?

But it was stupid of her to think he'd do anything different.

And he'd made no move towards Jem. Just that tight little smile. Unlike Rob, who'd given Jem plenty of hugs and was looking after the boy as if he were his own.

'Thank you,' she said.

'How are you feeling?'

How do you think *I'm feeling?* she wanted to yell. But she mustered up a smile. 'I'm doing OK. Rob's been brilliant.'

That one definitely hit home. To the outside world, Nick Tremayne looked the way he always did. But Kate knew him well enough to be able to read his eyes. A flash of guilt, there, that he'd left someone else to do his job. Supporting Jem.

'Good, good.' Nick shuffled awkwardly. 'Well, it was just a fleeting visit. I know you'll be tired and I don't want to... intrude.'

Kate knew she ought to be nice. Tell him it was fine. But after the way he'd let Jem down—and her—repeatedly, she didn't think he deserved to be let off the hook. 'Thanks for coming in. Give my love to everyone at the practice.' She refrained from adding that Polly had probably already done so.

'When are you coming out?'

'Tomorrow morning,' she said.

'I, um, might call in and see how you're doing, then.'

What did he expect? That she'd be overflowing with gratitude? 'If you have time,' she said. 'I know how busy things are.'

'Right. Well, look after yourself.' He stood there, holding the flowers. 'I'd better find a vase, or something.'

'I'll do that,' Rob said quietly, and held out his hand.

Kate noticed the look between them. And she also noticed that Nick was the first to look away, and simply gave the flowers to Rob.

James and Charlotte grew closer over the next few days. To his pleasure, she actually had lunch with him twice more. They talked mainly about work, but at least she was spending time with him. And James knew he wouldn't have traded a bacon roll and a mug of tea in the hospital canteen for the kind of five-course dinner and vintage Chateau Lafite in a Michelin-starred restaurant he'd shared with Sophia.

If anyone asked her, he was pretty sure she'd deny that they were dating. And technically they weren't: they were having a case conference during lunch.

But—and it was a big but—she didn't pull away when his foot rested against hers under the table, or when his fingers brushed against hers. Or when he kissed her goodbye in the corridor. Little by little, she was letting him closer.

It was enough to give him the confidence to try the next stage in his plan to show her that life could be fun.

'What do you think of the tie?' he asked in the middle of their next case conference.

'A teddy bear with a stethoscope?' She considered it. 'You'll have all the littlies smiling.'

It wasn't the littlies he wanted to make smile. It was her. 'Good. Something else I wanted to try out... Oh, what's that behind your ear, Dr Walker?'

'My ear?' She put her hand up to her head. 'There isn't anything.'

'Yes, there is. Say the magic word.' When she looked at him in puzzlement, he prompted, 'Abraca...?'

'Dabra,' she finished, rolling her eyes.

He grinned, held both palms up to prove his hands were empty, then reached behind her ear and produced a small gold box.

'How did you do that?' she asked.

'Magic.'

'Magic doesn't exist.'

Oh, yes, it did. 'Sleight of hand,' he said.

'Do that to your patients, and they'll adore you.'

He wanted *her* to adore him. 'Don't you want to know what's in the box?'

'No.'

'Don't tell fibs.' He dabbed his finger on the tip of her nose. 'You know what happened to Pinocchio.'

'You're saying I have a big nose?'

'No.' She had a beautiful nose. 'C'mon, Charlotte, you know you're itching to know what's in the box.'

'More like, you're itching to tell me,' she said dryly. But at least she was smiling. 'All right. I'll play. What's in the box, James?'

'Close your eyes.'

She looked wary. 'Why?'

'Because I asked you to. And you trust me, don't you?'

'Ye-es.'

'Close your eyes,' he said softly.

She did.

'Open your mouth.'

She opened her eyes instead. 'James, I'm not comfortable with this.'

'Trust me.' He looked intently at her. 'If you're worrying that I'm going to leap on you and kiss you, rest assured that I'm not.'

Something he didn't quite understand flickered in her eyes. 'You don't want to kiss me.'

It was a statement rather than a question. And delivered so flatly that he couldn't even begin to guess what she was thinking.

'Of course I want to kiss you. Oh, what the hell.' He dropped the box on her desk and took both her hands in his, drawing them up to his mouth. 'I know you're a very private person, so I'm not going to push you to explain why you're so wary of me. But I like you, and I think you like me, and for your information I've been having X-rated dreams about you for the last week.'

Colour stained her cheeks. 'James, I…'

Too far. Too fast. He knew he needed to reassure her. 'So, yes, Charlotte, I'd like to kiss you. Properly. Except we're in your office, and I know you'd hate it if anyone came in and caught us.'

She nodded.

'And that is the reason why I'm not planning to kiss you right this second.' His gaze held hers. 'Though rest assured that I'm going to kiss you properly. When you're ready and when it's the right time.'

He knew he'd said the right thing when she stopped holding her breath.

And he also knew that he needed to bring the subject back to work, so she'd believe that he was sincere about not rushing her. 'Now stop talking, close your eyes and open your mouth, because I'm due in Theatre in five minutes and I haven't got time to mess about.'

As he'd hoped, the mention of work calmed her down, and she followed his instructions. He opened the box, withdrew the chocolate and slid it into her mouth.

Her eyes opened and she stared at him. As she ate the chocolate, the wariness in her face melted. 'I wasn't expecting that,' she said when she'd finished.

'I know.' He grinned. 'Did you like it?'

She nodded.

'It's called "having fun",' he said softly. 'Work's important. But it's also important to play.' He brushed his mouth lightly against hers, the way he usually did after lunch. 'I'm off to Theatre. See you later.'

Charlotte watched him leave, pressing her fingertips against her mouth as she remembered what he said—and wondering.

What would it be like when James Alexander kissed her *properly*?

'You know,' Steffie said thoughtfully on Monday morning, 'I haven't seen you this smiley and relaxed before. A proper smile that goes all the way through you.'

'Don't be daft,' Charlotte said. 'Course you have.'

'Hmm.' Steffie didn't sound convinced. 'Well, there's something different about you. You seem…happier.'

Because she and James were—well, not seeing each other officially, but they were more than just friends.

Not that she was ready yet to admit it to anyone else.

'I enjoy my job, I love working with you lot, and the centre's about to open officially. Of course I'm happy,' Charlotte said.

Though Steffie had a point. She could feel herself smiling more often. And she knew why: simply because James was around. There was something about him that made her want to smile. For all the right reasons.

On Tuesday afternoon, James said to Charlotte, 'So you're not in tomorrow.'

'No.' She paused. 'Actually, the hospital trust has been really good. They've let me reschedule my hours and my patients don't miss out because my afternoon clinics start half an hour earlier and last for an hour longer, I do my ward rounds an hour later and then I do my admin.' She looked levelly at him. 'Knowing the hospital grapevine, I imagine you've already heard what I do on Wednesdays.'

'Something to do with a rape crisis centre.'

'Advice and counselling. I've been really lucky because Nick's letting me use a room at his practice. In return I do the odd heart health session in their well-woman clinic, and I've said if they want me to check anyone out while I'm there, that's absolutely fine.'

'That's pretty selfless of you.'

'It's the point of medicine,' Charlotte said. 'Giving something back and making people feel better.'

'True.'

'And I want to make a difference.'

He nodded. 'Well, obviously I'm not the right person to man a helpline or what have you—but if there's anything I can do to help, give me a shout.'

'Actually, I was thinking about sorting out a promise auction or something like that to raise funds—then we can train volunteers on the helpline and pay counsellors. The centre's all about being a free service.'

'Count me in to donate a promise, then. And if you want a hand organising it, I'm pretty good at that.'

She raised an eyebrow. 'You're good at organising?'

'My parents excel at organisation—and I think it's in my genes as well,' he said with a shrug.

'So you'd help with the centre?'

'I respect what you're doing and I respect you so, yes, I'd like to help.'

She gave him the sweetest smile. 'Thank you. I might just take you up on that.'

On Wednesday, Charlotte took a call that broke her heart. A young girl who'd gone through exactly the same thing that she had. Though Libby hadn't reported it at the time, thinking nobody would believe her, she'd been feeling worse and worse and worse. And she'd been at the point of doing something stupid when she'd seen an article about the centre.

Charlotte stayed talking to her for a long, long time. Listened. Made no judgements, just gave suggestions and advice about how to start the long journey back to feeling safe again.

And when she'd persuaded Libby to come and see a counsellor, she knew that the young girl wasn't the only one who'd taken a step on the road to recovery. She, too, was starting to heal properly.

On Friday, James perched on Charlotte's desk with a broad smile. 'I've had the most brilliant idea.'

'What sort of brilliant idea?'

'You know the quiz nights—we have ten teams, right?'

'Ye-es.'

'Well, I was thinking, maybe we could do something a bit different. Something I did in London that made a ton of money for the hospital.'

'Flashy stuff?' she asked wryly.

He sighed. 'Yes, I like glitz and glamour—and there's nothing wrong with liking a bit of flashy stuff, before you start nagging—but I also enjoy taking the chance to raise the profile of a good cause. I used to help raise a lot of money for the hospital in London, and I'd like to do that here, too.'

She could see that he was being sincere. 'So what did you have in mind?'

'A ball—say, in a month from now. We can raise money from ticket sales, and we'll run a tombola on the night.' His eyes sparkled. 'It'll be a ball with a difference—dinner, and then a dance competition. Ten pairs of dancers—one from each department, and the winning couple can choose where the money goes.'

As he spoke, Charlotte grew colder and colder. 'A dance.'

'What do you think? Will you help me organise it?'

Her last date had been a dance. With Michael. A night that had turned out to be the worst night of her life.

But she really didn't want to tell James about that. She didn't want to see pity or revulsion on his face. This thing between them was so new, so fragile, she didn't want to spoil that. Besides, she would be organising a ball, not actually dancing, so she could cope with it. And maybe facing it would help her overcome the last few hurdles.

'Charlotte?' he asked.

'Sorry, wool-gathering.' She nodded. 'All right, I'll help you.'

'Good. So we're on the same team this time.'

'I suppose so.'

He smiled. 'Excellent. So, do you know how to dance?'

'Dance?' He couldn't be serious. A sick feeling rose in her stomach.

'It's a ball. People dance at them.'

'But I won't have time to dance. I'm helping you organise it.'

'Mmm-hmm, but we can hand over the reins for five minutes while we dance—because I think we should be one of the teams. A cardio-surgery mix.'

He planned to dance…with her? Sickness turned to panic. 'No. Look, James, I don't dance.'

He spread his hands. 'Don't worry, I can teach you—I spent

too much of my misspent youth dancing.' He raised an eyebrow. 'Being flashy, you might say.'

She dug her nails into her palms underneath her desk, out of his sight. 'I can't do it, James.'

He really hadn't expected her to balk at this. Or to say she wasn't capable of doing something. The woman he'd come to know was quiet, yes, but she was hard-working and she didn't mess about. She simply got things done. 'Of course you can do it—besides, you're not on your own. We're a team. We're a good team at work, aren't we?'

'Ye-es.'

'So we'll be a good dance team, too. Trust me.'

'You're a doctor?' she capped.

He smiled, thinking all had to be well if she could be sassy with him.

'Something like that. So, where are we going to practise— your place or mine?'

'I…'

Why did she look so worried? 'Charlotte, I promise not to stand on your toes and make you hobble round the hospital for the next month.'

'No.' She paused. 'If we do this—and I mean if—we're not doing anything flashy like a tango.'

'No, of course not. I was thinking something like a waltz— especially as there was that Italian research showing that the waltz is one of the best ways to help regain cardiac function after a heart attack.'

Now that he'd put the subject back to medicine, she seemed to relax. 'The one where people who danced made better progress than those on an exercise bike?'

'They had a lower heart rate, higher lung capacity, and they also had more fun so were more likely to stick to the regime. And we can use that in the PR.'

'PR?' she queried.

'We tell the press what we're doing, they'll trail it in the local paper, and we'll get local businesses to offer prizes for the tombola. And we can double up when they contact us by asking them to donate something for your promise auction, too.'

'You don't hang about when you make a decision, do you?'

'No. Right—first lesson this evening, your place?'

'I…but you haven't organised it yet.'

He smiled. 'When I say I'll do something, I do it.'

'How are you going to book a band and food and what have you? It's summer, James. Everywhere's going to be booked up. You have to organise a ball *months* in advance—you're never going to do it in this short a time.'

'I like a challenge.'

The worry on her face seemed to deepen. James took a risk, squeezed her hand and let it go instantly. 'People aren't challenges, Charlotte. Tasks are. And I have contacts. I've done this sort of thing before, so it's not as if I'm going in cold.' Plus he could rope his parents in to help, if need be.

'Oh.' She looked a little less worried.

'What time tonight?'

'I…'

'Twenty minutes, that's all I'm asking,' he said softly. 'And that won't take much out of your evening. It'll still give you time to go and do whatever you normally do on a Friday night. Just tell me what time you want me to turn up—oh, and where you live.'

For a moment he thought she was going to back out. Then she nodded, still looking serious, and scribbled her address down on a piece of paper. 'Half past six, then. Do you need directions?'

'Thanks for the offer, but it won't be a problem.'

'Satnav, hmm?'

He smiled. 'See you at half past six.'

At precisely six-thirty Charlotte's doorbell rang. Trust James to be absolutely on time. She opened the door and discovered that he'd changed from his suit into jeans; somehow it made him feel less threatening, yet at the same time more dangerous. Touchable.

Though there was something else worrying her. 'Did the paparazzi follow you here?'

'No. They don't do it all the time.' He shrugged. 'And, anyway, they've decided I must be on a health kick because I cycle practically everywhere, so at the moment I'm not very interesting.'

She pushed away the thought of how interested the press would be at the idea of James Alexander giving his colleague private dance lessons. 'Come in. Can I get you a coffee or something cold?'

'Thanks, but I'm fine.'

She frowned. 'James, why are you whispering?'

'Because you told me your cat is nervous of men with loud voices, and I don't want to worry her.' He produced a small ball with a bell in it. 'I have to admit, I don't know much about cats, but the woman in the pet shop says they like these.'

'James, you really don't have to buy my cat a present—but thank you.' She led him into the living room. Pandora was sitting on the back of the sofa, her tail swishing; Charlotte picked up the cat and held her close. 'Pandora, this is James. He's a friend. It's OK,' she soothed, her voice calm and soft.

'As I said, don't know much about cats, but I'll work on the same principle as dogs—you don't crowd them and you let them come to check you out when they're ready,' James said.

She remembered what Melinda said about telling people's characters through their reactions to animals. James was giving the cat space, which meant he was likely to give her space, too. When the muscles between her shoulder blades eased, she realised just how tense she'd been.

'Now, are we going to do our routine to classical or pop?'

She grimaced. 'Sorry, I really hadn't even begun to think about this. I haven't done this sort of thing.' She'd made perfectly sure she was working on the night of the hospital ball, in the past, and people who'd wanted to go had been more than happy to exchange duties with her.

'Then humour me on this. I think we'll do classical.'

'So are you planning to have a huge orchestra?'

'A string quartet and a pop band,' he explained. 'I know a couple who owe me a favour, so it won't be a problem booking them.'

'I still can't believe you're going to organise this whole thing in less than a month.'

'*We* are,' he corrected. 'Tomorrow, I'll run the posters by you.'

He was planning to see her tomorrow?

'I'll call you,' he amended, clearly reading the surprise in her face. 'I'll read it through to you if you're busy.'

'OK.'

'Now, your first dance lesson. The waltz has just three steps—natural turn, reverse turn and change steps.' He demonstrated them for her. 'It's just a matter of following the beat and following my lead. Don't worry if you stand on my toes. I won't break.' He fished his mobile phone out of his pocket. 'Can I put this on the mantelpiece? It has a music player.'

It was one of the latest and most exclusive mobile phones around. It was odd, Charlotte thought, that this incredibly rich guy who mixed with the rich and famous would be slumming it in her little terrace in a Cornish seaside town. Then again, he was also James Alexander, children's heart surgeon, a man whose judgement she trusted at work. The only man she'd allowed to kiss her since Michael. So maybe this wasn't going to be so bad.

And then he manoeuvred her into the hold.

'James, isn't this a bit close?'

'That's the other reason I chose it. Because it means you're going to be close to me,' he said.

She dragged in a breath. 'I…'

'Charlotte, I'm not going to hurt you. Just dance with you. Relax,' he said softly. 'If I'm going too fast, we'll skip the music and do just the steps, until you get the hang of it.'

'Sorry.' She almost—*almost*—told him about Michael, but at the last moment she couldn't bring herself to do it. She didn't want James to look at her with pity or revulsion. So instead she concentrated on following his lead, trying not to stumble.

'We'll do one more track and then stop,' James said.

She could still feel her heart racing, but he walked her through a three-minute waltz track, and this time it wasn't quite as hard.

'That's enough for today,' he said as the music stopped. He released one of her hands—but instead of taking a step backwards, he cupped her face. Bent his head to hers.

The fingers of her other hand were still tangled with his. And instead of pulling away from his kiss, she found herself responding.

And, to her mingled shock and delight, it was good.

When he broke the kiss, his pupils were huge and his colour had heightened. 'Charlotte. I wasn't expecting…' He stroked her cheek with the pad of his thumb. 'Thank you,' he said softly.

And he was the one to step back. To give her space.

'I said I'd take twenty minutes of your evening. Sorry, I've already gone past that. I'll leave now and let you get on.'

He really wasn't going to crowd her.

And she appreciated that. Enough to make a gesture of her own. 'If you're really not doing anything this evening, you can stay and have something to eat if you like. Nothing fancy, just baked salmon and new potatoes and salad.'

'If you're sure, I'd love that.' He smiled at her. 'Tell me where the nearest off-licence is, and I'll go and get some wine to go with it.'

'No need. I've got a couple of bottles in the rack; I can stick one in the fridge.' She paused. 'Did you cycle over?'

'No, I drove. So maybe I'll take a rain check on the wine.' He gave her a naughty little boy grin. 'Want to come and see my car?'

'Your James Bond car?' Something about the mischief in his eyes warmed her. 'You were kidding me, weren't you? It's a complete rust-bucket.'

'Come and see.'

She did.

And it wasn't.

It really was a shiny, gleaming, silver Aston Martin.

'James Bond.' She bit her lip. 'Are you sure you want to leave your car there?'

'Apart from the fact this is hardly a rough area, it's just a car. A box on four wheels.'

Er, no. It was a seriously expensive sports car, and you had to be on a waiting list to get one.

He gave her a sidelong look. 'Or there's another option.'

'What's that?'

'It'll take you about thirty minutes to cook salmon and new potatoes, yes?'

'Yes.'

'How far away is the nearest chip shop?'

'About five minutes.'

'Right. So that's twenty minutes to drive up the coast and back to your chip shop, five minutes to queue, and five minutes to get back here. How about it?'

She looked longingly at the car. It was hugely tempting. 'James, aren't you worried that the fish and chips will make your car smell?'

'We're not eating in the car,' he pointed out, 'and I'll have the windows open. So, no. Come and have some fun with me, Charlotte.'

This time, she didn't think about it. Didn't stop to check if there were any paparazzi around. She just gave in to the impulse. 'Let me lock my front door, and you're on.'

Driving in his car was just fabulous. It made her feel like a film star; no wonder he loved his car so much.

'Next time we have a teenage boy in, you can tell him you've sat in my James Bond car,' he said.

'It would be better still if I told him I'd actually driven it,' she retorted.

'He wouldn't believe you—James Bond wouldn't let a woman drive his car.'

She laughed. 'And now you're being sexist.'

'You want to drive?' He pulled over, removed the keys and tossed them to her.

She caught them automatically. 'James! I—No. Supposing I crash?'

'You won't crash.'

'Or scrape it? Or dent it? Or—?'

'Charlotte, it's a only a car,' he interrupted.

'It's gleaming. You must polish it every single day.'

'Well, yes,' he admitted.

She shook her head. 'I can't do this.'

'You thought you couldn't dance,' he pointed out. 'Yet you danced with me tonight.'

And kissed him back. 'That was different.'

He smiled. 'Not so very different. It's just a matter of confidence.' He glanced at his watch. 'Actually, we'd better get going or we'll be late for the chips.'

Just as he'd promised, they were back at her house within the half-hour.

'Thank you,' Charlotte said softly, when he finally got up to leave.

'What for?'

'Being patient with me. I didn't expect that.'

'It's not my strong suit, I admit,' James said. 'But I'm happy to try.'

'I'm happy to try, too,' Charlotte said.

'Thank you,' James said. And when he kissed her goodbye

in the hallway, Charlotte felt safe enough with him to return the kiss.

Because James was most definitely different.

CHAPTER NINE

THREE weeks after her lumpectomy, Kate had her first radio-therapy session. She'd already met the radiology team, who'd marked tiny dots on her skin to show the area where she'd need treatment, and they'd advised her not to use any perfumed shower gel, deodorant or talcum powder because it might make her skin sore: plain soap and aqueous cream would be better.

'I know your appointment's not until eleven,' Rob said, 'but if we leave at ten, that allows us plenty of time for traffic. And we can always go and have something in the café if we're really early.'

Kate hugged him. 'I really appreciate this, Rob.'

'I know. And I also know you'd do the same for me, so don't start getting any silly ideas.' He hugged her back. 'You don't have to worry about Jem, love. We'll wait with you until you're called in, and then we'll go for a walk or the boys will play on their consoles. And then we'll play it by ear—see how you feel. If you're tired, we'll go home, I'll make you a sandwich and you can sit with your feet up while I take the boys swimming; if you're feeling OK, maybe we can do something together.'

As a family.

The idea warmed her.

'Have I told you lately that you're wonderful?' she asked.

'Yes,' he said with a grin, 'but I'm quite happy for you to keep telling me.'

* * *

On Wednesday night, James didn't turn up at their usual time for their dance lesson. Charlotte tried his mobile, but it was switched over to voicemail; she didn't bother leaving a message, assuming that he was on his way and kept his phone switched to voicemail while he was driving.

When another hour had passed, she tried again. Still voicemail. 'James, this is Charlotte. I'm assuming that you can't make it this evening,' she said. She hung up and made herself a coffee. When she still hadn't heard from James half an hour later, she was about to give up waiting and run herself a bath, then her doorbell rang.

When she opened the door, James stood there, looking drawn. 'You look terrible,' she said.

'I feel it,' he admitted. 'I've been in Theatre all day.'

'Come and sit down. What's happened?'

He sank onto the sofa. 'The special care unit called me. They delivered a baby last night with a narrowed aortic valve—Tom. He wasn't up to surgery, so he was in ICU while they hoped to get him a bit stronger. He was cyanotic, and oxygen and prostaglandin therapy didn't do much. So that left me as his best chance. Let's just say it was a bit tricky.' He sighed. 'I did try to ring you, but your phone was engaged.'

'I'm sorry.' She sat down beside him and took his hand. 'Let's skip the lesson tonight. You look shattered—and I bet you haven't eaten, have you?'

'Well, no,' he admitted. 'I was too busy. And I've gone past hunger.'

'And your blood sugar will be dropping like a stone. Stay there and I'll fix you something,' she said.

'Really, you don't have to,' he protested.

'It's going to take me five minutes to make you an omelette. No big deal. Stay put.' She left to pour him a glass of orange juice, then went back into the living room. 'Have this for now. I'll call you when it's ready.'

But when she slid the omelette onto the plate, there was no

answer. She walked through to the living room, and James had simply fallen asleep where he sat. And, to her surprise, Pandora was curled up on his lap.

He must be exhausted, she thought, deciding not to wake him. 'Good girl. Stay there,' she whispered to the cat, and tiptoed back out into the kitchen.

Half an hour later, James's mobile phone rang, and he woke with a start. He was even more shocked to find Pandora curled up on his lap. Since when…? And he couldn't even remember falling asleep.

He grabbed the phone from his pocket. 'James Alexander.'

'James, it's Rita from SCBU. We need you back in Theatre, I'm afraid,' the nurse told him. 'Tom isn't doing too well.'

'On my way,' James said. Gently, he stroked Pandora. 'Sorry, Puss. I'm going to have to move you.' He scooped her up and stood up just as Charlotte walked into the living room. 'Sorry, got to go back to Theatre.'

'Tom?' she asked.

He nodded bleakly. 'And you made me dinner and I wasted it. Sorry.'

'James, it was only an omelette. Look, I'll make you a sandwich to go while you wash your face to wake up a bit.' She took Pandora from him. 'Come on, you. Let the poor man go. Bathroom's top of the stairs, right in front of you,' she said.

When he came down after splashing his face, she'd wrapped up a sandwich for him. 'Take care. I'll see you tomorrow,' she said softly. And then she really shocked him by taking the lead and kissing him. The warmth and sweetness stayed with him all the way through a tough evening in Theatre, and all the way back to his office. And when he closed his eyes to drift into sleep, it was Charlotte's face he saw.

The following morning, Charlotte was sorting out her paper-work before clinic when there was a knock at her door.

She'd never seen James look like that before. His hair was

unkempt, his face—usually clean-shaven—was covered with stubble, and his clothes were creased. 'James?' she asked.

'Sorry. I feel rubbish.'

He looked it.

'I know it's completely inappropriate of me to ask, but I could really do with a hug.'

To her horror, she could actually see tears in his eyes. Something had happened. Something awful. Immediately, she walked over to him and wrapped her arms round him. 'What's wrong? Has something happened with your family?'

'No.' He swallowed hard and rested his head against her shoulder. 'Just, sometimes, I hate my job.'

'What's *happened*, James?'

He dragged in a breath. 'You know I came back to Theatre last night—well, I stayed here last night, in case I was needed.'

That explained his dishevelled appearance.

'And Tom died, Charlotte. I couldn't save him. I let him down, I let his parents down, and I let the team down.'

'Hey. You did your best—if you couldn't do it, nobody else could.'

'It doesn't feel like it right now.'

'You're a good surgeon. And I should know, because I've seen you work.'

'I don't lose many patients.' He held her closer. 'But it hurts like hell when I do. I was meant to save people, Charlotte, not lose them.'

She stroked his hair back from his forehead. 'Listen to me. You were in Theatre all day yesterday and most of the evening. And where did you sleep last night?'

'The chair in my office,' he admitted.

'Which meant you got practically no sleep.'

'I cat-napped.' He shrugged. 'But that's par for the course, a skill a surgeon has to learn early on.' He shivered. 'I hate my job, Charlotte. I really hate it when it doesn't work and I have to make the call. I hate it when I have to say the words "time of death". I hate having to tell the parents I couldn't save their child and I see the light go out in their eyes—when I see the grief and desperation just seeping through them, and *I should've been able to stop it happening.*' The last words came out overlaid with pain.

'You're being way too hard on yourself, James.' Her heart ached for him, but at the same time she was glad he'd confided in her, had taken off the mask of the flash playboy doctor and let her see the man underneath. He was a good man, who was hurting—a man who needed her.

She had no idea how long she stayed there, just holding him, letting her strength prop him up. But one thing she was sure about: if the positions had been reversed, James would be holding her and he'd be the strong one, letting her lean on him.

He'd once told her that they'd make a fabulous team.

And she had a feeling that he was right.

The week before the ball, James asked Charlotte to come over to his place for the dance lesson. 'Not that there's anything wrong with your place, but we need to try our routine in a larger area.'

'And your place is huge, right?'

'It's rented, so it's not strictly my place,' he said, 'but… um…yes. It's pretty big.'

That barely described it, Charlotte thought when he ushered her inside. The living room took up the entire top floor of the three-storey house—an enormous expanse with a sea view, a balcony and a proper wooden floor. Not to mention a state-of-the-art audio-visual system and enormous, butter-soft leather sofas.

Funny how far they'd come in four weeks. Four weeks of working together, dancing together, sharing bits of each other's lives. To the point where she'd even kiss him in her office, not worrying that someone might spot them and start gossiping. Four weeks ago, when she'd first danced with him, she'd stumbled over everything. And now she was gliding with him, at one with him, practically feeling his heart beat in time with hers.

He switched on his sound system and the first notes of the waltz from Tchaikovsky's *Sleeping Beauty* floated into the air. As they began dancing, she realised that he was right. Even with the furniture pushed back, her living room had been limited in space. Now they spun together and it was like floating. She actually closed her eyes, trusting in the rhythm of the music and James's lead. With one sense temporarily missing, the others grew more intense—she was aware of the hard muscle beneath her fingertips, the warmth of his hand in hers, his clean masculine scent.

At the very end, instinctively she tipped her face up towards his to welcome his kiss; her mouth tingled, her blood seemed to fizz in her veins, and she slid her hand from his shoulder to the back of his neck to pull him closer.

When they finally broke the kiss, they were both shaking.

'Charlotte. Stay with me tonight,' he said softly.

For a moment, she almost said yes. James was the first man she'd wanted to make love with since Michael—and she really did want to touch him, explore him, find out what gave him pleasure and what blew his mind. And let him explore her just the same way.

Though she knew it wasn't fair to take things further without telling him the truth about her past. Something that she wished now she'd done earlier, because she had no idea how he'd react. He'd be angry on her behalf, she knew that much, but when he'd had time to think about it, would it make him reject her?

'I…It's the wrong time of the month,' she prevaricated.

It wasn't true, but it was the best excuse she could think of right at that moment.

He brushed his mouth against hers. 'Stay anyway. You can still sleep in my arms. Even if I don't touch you the way I'm desperate to touch you.'

She really hadn't expected that sweetness from him. And it made her want to cry. 'James, I…'

'It's OK. I'm not going to rush you. I can wait until you're ready.' He dropped a kiss on her forehead and gently disengaged himself from the dance hold.

'Thank you,' she whispered.

'So have you decided on a dress yet?' he asked.

'No,' she admitted. She'd been so busy learning to dance that she'd forgotten about the dress. And she wasn't used to glitzy, glamorous clothes. She didn't go to glitzy, glamorous places— just on team nights out, to the bowling alley and to the cinema and to restaurants where casual clothing was perfectly acceptable. 'Sorry. I'll go and find something at the weekend.'

'Forgive me,' he said, 'for being a bit pushy.'

'Pushy?' she asked, not understanding.

'Stay where you are and close your eyes.' As if he sensed that she was about to ask why, he added with a smile, 'Humour me. It was OK last time, wasn't it?'

When he'd fed her chocolate. 'Uh-huh.' Warily, she did as he asked.

'Don't open your eyes or you'll spoil it,' he warned.

She heard him walk out of the room; a few moments later, she heard him ask, 'Are your eyes still closed?'

'Yes.'

There was a rustling sound. 'You can open your eyes now.'

She did so, and blinked in a mixture of surprise and delight as she saw the most incredible dress hanging on the door. 'Wow.' Then she bit her lip. 'James, that's a really lovely gesture, but this must have cost a fortune.'

He shrugged it off. 'As I said, I've been a bit pushy, but I really wanted to buy you a proper ballroom dancing dress. Do you mind very much?'

'*Mind?* James, it's *beautiful.* Thank you.' The dress was cornflower blue, the skirt was ankle length, silky and swirly, and the top was strappy. There was a floaty strip of silk running from the shoulder to a small cuff on her wrist; the back was low, but it wasn't the glittery thing she would've expected him to choose. It was subtle, and beautiful, and incredibly feminine. 'It's like a fairy princess dress.'

'Well, we're dancing to the *Sleeping Beauty* waltz. I thought the dress went with the song.'

She smiled. 'I'm fairly sure it was Cinderella who had a blue dress, not Sleeping Beauty, and from memory it was a much paler blue.'

He laughed. 'This one's the same colour as your eyes. That's why I chose it.'

He'd noticed the colour of her eyes?

And then another thought hit her. 'How did you know what size to buy?'

'Guesswork,' he said. 'Bearing in mind what my mother did for a living, it's something I picked up from her, not because I'm a leering Lothario who sizes up every female in my path. But it *is* a guess, and that's why I'm giving it to you now, in case it needs alterations. If you want to try it on, my bedroom's down the stairs, first door you see.'

His bedroom.

She felt the colour flood into her face.

'Uh, that came out wrong,' he said hastily. 'We've already established that we're not sharing a bedroom tonight. What I meant was, you can change in the bathroom if you want, or use my room if you want somewhere with a full-length mirror. And I'll be on the balcony if you want to come and see me when you're dressed.'

He really was trying, she thought. Really wasn't taking it for granted that she'd be like all the women in his past. 'Thank you,' she said softly. On impulse, she walked over to him, and kissed him on the cheek. 'For—well. Lots of things.'

'Go and try the dress on.' He flapped a hand at her. 'Before I try to change your mind.'

The back of the dress was much lower than she was used to,

but it also meant she could handle the zip herself. And it fitted perfectly. She took her hair out of the French pleat she usually wore it in and let it fall over her bare shoulders.

'You look amazing,' he said when she joined him on the balcony. 'Turn round, so I can see it properly.'

'Obviously I'll get proper shoes,' she said. 'With heels the same height as the ones I've been using when we've practised.'

He nodded. 'And spray the soles with hairspray. It's another of my mother's tips—it means you're less likely to slip on the floor.' Almost as if unable to help himself, he curled the ends of her hair round his fingers. 'Your hair is beautiful like that,' he said softly, 'but it's easier to dance with it up. Just leave a couple of curls at the front to soften it.'

It sounded almost as if he was voicing a personal dream. Dangerous—so she took refuge in sass. 'And lots of glitter and make-up?'

He laughed. 'You don't need it.'

'I wasn't fishing.'

'I know.' His fingers were still in her hair. And her knees were decidedly wobbly. 'And you're wearing what?'

'An ordinary black tailcoat and trousers.'

She knew he was understating it—his outfit would be beautifully cut and hideously expensive—but that was who James was, what he'd grown up with. She had to learn to accept that about him.

'So shall we give it a whirl?'

They went through their routine again, and with the dress it made everything feel much more real. And she felt exactly like the fairy princess in the tale.

At the end, he kissed her again. A sweet, slow kiss that made her bones melt. And then he took a step back. 'Just so I can keep my promise to be a gentleman,' he said softly.

'OK, love?' Rob settled Kate onto the sofa.

'Just tired. I really didn't expect it to hit me like this,' she admitted. 'I know women who've had radiotherapy in their coffee breaks.'

'And others who've been sick as well as tired. Look on the bright side—you've been spared that.' He fetched her a glass of water. 'I'm just sorry that I have to go back to work next week and can't take you to the rest of your sessions.'

'Rob, you've spent your entire summer holidays looking after me. You've taken me to three weeks of radiotherapy,' she said, 'and you've been brilliant with the boys. You've had them doing chores without complaining, taken them out to burn off all that energy, and you've done more than your fair share of the cooking. I…I just can't tell you how much I appreciate it.' She scrubbed at a tear. 'And how much I hate being weepy and maudlin like this. It isn't *me*.'

'I know that, love.' He leaned over to kiss her. 'It's the radiotherapy, making you feel tired and a bit low. And, besides, tears can be healing.' He smiled wryly.

'Everyone's been so kind.' Kate indicated the vases of flowers that filled the room—and there were just as many in the kitchen. 'Every day someone brings me flowers.' To the point where Rob had had to nip out and buy some extra vases. As soon as one vase had passed its best and she'd consigned them to the compost heap, within half an hour someone else would bring some in. 'Polly's been brilliant.' She'd dropped in every day. 'And everyone from the practice.' Except Nick. Once he'd learned that Rob had moved in, he'd gone for complete avoidance. And Kate was surprised how much it still hurt.

'That's because,' Rob said, 'everyone loves you. And my guess is you've supported them in the past. And what goes around comes around. I think you're amazing, and so do the boys.'

'You're pretty amazing yourself, Robert Werrick.'

He brushed the compliment aside. 'So who's taking you to the hospital next week? Because I warn you, Kate, if you're even *thinking* about driving yourself, I'm going to confiscate your car keys.'

'No, I'm not,' she reassured him. 'Polly's already organised a rota, bless her. I was so worried about her, especially as this happened right at the time she came back and I haven't been there to support her. She's so strong in many ways, but still so fragile in others.'

'Kate, don't feel guilty. I'm sure she understands.'

'She more than understands, bless her. She's set it up so that she, Oliver, Dragan, Gabriel and Chloe are all doing one day a week, so that's the two weeks covered.'

'And the boys are both going to football training after school on the days when I'm doing after-school triathlon coaching,' he said. 'So you don't have to worry about them—I'll pick them up from their school when I've finished coaching at mine. Everything's going to be just fine.'

And Kate was beginning to believe him.

On Saturday morning, Charlotte dropped in to see Melinda. 'Oh, just look at them! They're gorgeous,' she said when she saw the puppies curled up asleep next to their mother. 'Bramble, you're such a clever girl.'

The flatcoat retriever's tail thumped.

'So how old are they now?'

'Twelve days. They can see now,' Melinda explained, 'but they can't hear yet.'

'Would Bramble mind if I...?'

'She's used to people dropping in now,' Melinda said with a smile.

Charlotte made a fuss of Bramble, then gently stroked one of the pups. 'So soft. Do you have homes lined up for them all yet?'

'I have a few people interested,' Melinda said, 'though they won't be ready until near the end of October. Kate said she'd like one of the brown ones for Jem; if she's not feeling quite up to dealing with a pup at that point, we'll look after him for a bit longer. We want to keep one ourselves.'

'Could you put me down for one of the black ones?' Charlotte asked.

'Anything to do with a certain person you think might be good with children and animals?' Melinda asked.

'Maybe,' Charlotte said. 'He did say something to me about wanting a dog when he was a boy.'

'Ah. You know, I'll have to meet him first—and I won't be vetting him for you. I'll be vetting him for the pup.'

Charlotte laughed. 'Of course. Though, if it helps, Pandora makes a beeline for him whenever he comes over and sprawls all over him.'

'That's a good sign. So you're seeing him?' Melinda asked.

'I'm his dance partner at the charity ball.'

'But it's more than that, *cara*?'

Charlotte gave a shy nod.

'*Bene*. I thought so. He's chased away a lot of the shadows in your eyes. And don't deny it. My Dragan's the same,' Melinda said with a gentle smile.

'Do you think a pup would get on with Pandora?'

'The wind's blowing in that direction, *cara*?'

'Too early to say. But just supposing…?'

'Burmese blues are pretty sociable,' Melinda said thoughtfully. 'I know Pandora had a bad scare when her owner died, but she's very settled with you. Obviously it'd take a few days for them to settle in together, but it's a lot easier to introduce a pup into a house with an adult cat than it is to introduce a kitten into a house with an adult dog. I'd say you'd be fine.'

On Monday morning, James knocked on Charlotte's office door. 'Got a minute?'

'Sure.'

He closed the door behind him, pulled the blinds, then drew her to her feet and kissed her thoroughly. 'Mmm. That's better.

I've got some good news—I've managed to get the judges I wanted for the ball.' He named some dancers that even Charlotte had heard of.

'How did you manage that?' she asked.

'By shamelessly asking some of my mother's friends,' he said with a grin. 'Anyway, we're definitely going to have the nationals covering us now.'

'Nationals?'

'Press. Which means we'll get money coming in after the event.'

The national press.

Oh, no.

The last thing she wanted was the national press hanging around. Especially as someone might do some digging and connect her with a certain story from three years before…'I'd rather not, James.'

'Rather not what?' He looked mystified.

'Involve the national press. Look, this is a local thing. We don't need the papers from London. And it'd be better to get the hospital press office to handle it for us.'

'Charlotte, I've been dealing with the press for years. They'll love this.'

'I'd really rather not.' She took a deep breath. 'So if the papers are there, I won't be.'

'Why?'

'Because…' Now wasn't the right place to tell him about Michael and the court case. 'I prefer my life to be a bit more private.' She still had no idea how she and James had managed to avoid being photographed together. But as soon as the national press came down here…she and James would have no privacy at all.

And as for what it meant for the crisis centre…

'I don't want to be involved with the press,' she said.

'Charlotte. There's nothing to worry about, really. It'll be fine.' He pressed a kiss into her palm and folded her fingers round it. 'Look—'

But whatever he'd been going to say was interrupted by his bleeper. He checked the screen and grimaced. 'Sorry. Got to go.'

'But you'll let the hospital press office handle it? And stick to just talking to the local newspaper?' Charlotte asked. 'Please?'

'Don't worry,' he reassured her. 'I'll sort everything out. See you later.' He kissed her, and left her office.

Nobody at the hospital talked about anything else for the next few days except the ball. By Thursday, the entire place was buzzing. James and Charlotte had promised to go into the children's ward just beforehand to give their patients a preview of Charlotte's dress.

'Dr Charlotte, you look just like a princess!' Tammy, the patient James had operated on the previous week to close a hole in the heart, said. 'And Dr James looks like Prince Charming.'

In a black tailcoat and trousers, a white wingtip shirt and a white bow-tie, Charlotte thought that James looked stunning. In his top pocket there was a silk square the same colour as her dress; typical James, paying attention to all the details.

'You're going to win,' Tammy declared.

'Maybe,' Charlotte said with a smile. And maybe they were going to win something more important than a dance competition.

James had ordered them a limousine.

'Surely I'm allowed to be flashy tonight?' he teased.

'Hmm,' Charlotte said, though she couldn't help smiling. He looked as excited as a little boy who'd just been told he could pick anything he liked from a toyshop.

At the ball, James was in his element—compering, persuading people to buy extra tombola tickets, smiling at everyone.

And he'd really pulled off the organisation. He had friends

in TV who'd lent them special machines for the evening so that the audience could vote for their favourite dancers. He'd lined up four judges—Geoff Hunter, the head of surgery; Albert White, the hospital's chief executive; and the two professional dancers he'd told her about, who were happy to sign autographs and had donated tickets for top seats to their own shows as tombola prizes. The hospital's press officer was there, to Charlotte's relief; although they'd never had a chance to finish that conversation, clearly James had listened to her worries about the press.

She'd never seen her colleagues do all the glamorous stuff before—a huge variety of dances, from a passionate tango through to a glitzy American smooth—and everyone was clearly enjoying themselves.

She and James were the last couple to dance. When James picked up the microphone again to announce them, her heart started thumping so hard and so loudly that she was sure the people either side of her must be able to hear it.

'The cardio-surgical team has opted for a waltz,' James said, 'because there's research proof that it's good for your heart. We're just practising what we preach.' He handed the microphone over to Geoff.

'Ladies and gentlemen,' Geoff said as James walked over to Charlotte, 'I give you the cardio-surgical team, Charlotte Walker and James Alexander.'

The cheering and clapping fuelled her nerves even more.

'Stop panicking,' James said in a low voice. 'We're going to do just fine. We've done this every single day for the last month, and you know it works. Just pretend we're dancing in your living room and Pandora's watching us.'

'OK.' But in her head she was thinking about dancing with him in that huge room overlooking the sea, and the way he'd kissed her.

And then she heard the first notes of the song: she and James were under the spotlight, waltzing, and it felt as though she were floating. At the very end, James was kissing her. Really kissing her. And it was only the sound of the applause that reminded her where they were and brought her to her senses.

Just.

The judges delivered their verdicts. Three nines—and a ten, which sent James straight into Cheshire cat mode.

'Don't forget it's the audience vote that counts,' James said, taking the microphone back. 'Think about it while we have dinner and a dance ourselves, and we're going to announce the winner right at the very end.'

CHAPTER TEN

THE rest of the evening was a blur. Although Charlotte danced with other colleagues, she didn't get the floaty feeling with them that she'd experienced in James's arms. Every time she danced with James, it was as if all the lights were brighter and all the sparkly bits were glitzier. And to her surprise nobody teased her about that incredibly public kiss. Steffie just gave her a hug and whispered, 'We all guessed that was the way things were going, and you make a fabulous couple. I'm so glad for you.'

And then it was time for the final announcement. Charlotte was expecting it to go to Lisa and Matt, who'd danced the tango incredibly professionally. But then James's TV friend finished totting up the votes, and whispered to Albert White.

The chief exec made a mercifully short speech, and then smiled. 'I'm delighted to announce that the winning couple is the cardio-surgical team.'

Charlotte was too stunned to say a word. All she could do was follow James as he took her hand and tugged her along beside him.

'This is a first,' James said. 'I'm used to Charlotte being quiet, but not speechless. Thank you very much for voting for us, and I hope you've had as good a time this evening as we have. Your generosity has helped us raise a huge amount of money...' there were gasps when he named the amount '...and

I'd like to split it between three very deserving causes. Firstly, to the Friends of the Hospital, because they really do make a difference; secondly, to the cardiac department at St Piran's; and, thirdly, to the rape crisis centre that my brilliant dance partner has set up in Penhally. Thank you all very much.'

Flashbulbs were going off everywhere, there was so much noise that Charlotte could barely make out a word anyone was saying to her—and she was completely overwhelmed.

She hadn't expected this at all. She'd assumed that if they won—and she'd doubted that—James would want to split the money between the Friends of the Hospital and maybe the cath lab. But he'd put the spotlight on the rape crisis centre.

He hadn't given her the vaguest hint—and that showed her just how little she really did know him. Although part of her was delighted to know there was money coming in to help train volunteers for the helpline and to pay for counselling sessions for those who needed them, she still couldn't get past the fact that James hadn't even discussed it with her first.

He'd been completely high-handed about it.

And those flashbulbs… They had to be more than just the local papers. Even knowing that she didn't want the nationals there, he'd just gone straight ahead with what he wanted.

So much for thinking that he was nothing like Michael. He, too, had completely ignored her requests.

She was so hurt and angry that she couldn't say a word.

'What's wrong?' James asked, a few minutes later when she still hadn't said much.

'Bit of a headache.' It wasn't a complete fib. There was a tight, nagging band around her forehead.

'I'll take you home,' he said.

She shook her head. 'No need. You've got things to sort out here. I'll get a taxi.'

'Sure?'

'Sure.' The quicker she was out of there, the better. Before she said something unforgivable to him. She needed time to cool down.

'I'll call you later,' he said.

'I'd rather you didn't.'

'Of course. You need some sleep to get rid of that headache. Just text me when you get in, so I know you're home safely. And I'll see you tomorrow,' he said.

Except the following morning turned out to be even more difficult. When Charlotte rounded the corner to go into the hospital, she saw a pack of people waiting outside the main entrance.

As she drew closer, she could see cameras. And all of a sudden the pack turned and surged towards her. Flashbulbs popped, people were calling her name and yelling out questions, all talking at once. Instinctively, she raised her hand to her face and pushed her way through the crowd, not saying a word.

She'd seen this kind of thing in films and on television, but never in real life. All this, just because she'd won a dance competition in a charity ball? Ridiculous.

People in the corridor glanced at her curiously; some nudged others and whispered and pointed.

It wasn't until she passed the hospital shop and saw the newspaper stand that she realised what was really going on.

PLAYBOY DOC DANCES INTO HER HEART
DOCTOR KISSES PLAYBOY BETTER

She stared at the headlines in disbelief. One of the papers even had a photograph of her dancing with James, showing that kiss at the end.

Oh, no. How *could* she have been so stupid? Even when they'd had a quiet dinner in the pub, they'd been snapped by the press. She should've realised that this sort of thing would happen. That even if it had just been the local papers there, the press would ignore the story about the money they'd raised and focus on James's personal life. And as the nationals were there…

This was bad.

She glanced quickly through the papers. At least there was nothing about Liverpool. For now. But it wouldn't take long for the press to dig it up. She'd wanted to stop Michael hurting someone else and to get help for him, so she'd agreed to waive her right to anonymity and she'd been named in the press. Bitter as it had felt at the time, she'd done it for the greater good. To make sure that justice was done.

Nobody in St Piran knew what had happened in Liverpool. She hadn't talked about it even to Steffie or Tim, the colleagues she was closest to, and when they found out the truth, they'd be so hurt that she'd shut them out.

But it hadn't been like that.

She'd wanted a fresh start, that was all. Somewhere that her name wasn't known. She'd been so happy here; and now it was going to be spoiled. Instead of people seeing the young, capable doctor they'd worked with for nearly two years, they'd see a victim.

And maybe the whispers would go out that she'd led him on, that date rape wasn't as bad as raping a stranger. But in her view, if anything, it was worse when someone you trusted betrayed you and hurt you like that.

The newspapers would get their angle and it wouldn't be the truth. There would be some kind of spin on it. Hadn't James himself said that the press always exaggerated their stories about him?

But even that paled into comparison with the real damage the stories would do. How would anyone at the centre trust her now? How could she give quiet support to people who needed it, people who were vulnerable? The last thing they needed was the press sniffing round and blaring lurid headlines about rape.

There was only one way to keep herself safe—to keep the

people who came to the centre for help safe—and that was to back off from James.

Right now.

There were murmurs and looks when she walked onto the ward, and she hated it. Even Steffie looked wary. 'Are you all right, Charlotte?' she asked.

'I'm fine, thank you,' she said tightly.

'Hon, you don't look it.'

'I could throttle James,' Charlotte admitted. 'He didn't even discuss it with me.'

'Maybe he was trying to give you a nice surprise.'

'Maybe he wanted everyone to see what a hero he was,' Charlotte retorted, her lip curling.

'Charlotte—look, let me get you a cup of tea.'

'Thanks, but I'm fine.' And hanging around the department was making it worse. 'I'll be back in a minute. Bleep me if it's urgent.'

She stomped over to the surgical department and waited for James in his office. Her temper sizzled more with every passing second, and when James finally walked in she didn't give him a chance to speak. Even though she knew she was being unfair, that she was equally to blame, she lost her temper.

'What the *hell* were you thinking of?' she demanded. 'Look at the circus out there!'

'I'm s—' he began.

'Sorry? For pity's sake, James, why didn't you *think* before you opened your mouth? Women who've been raped don't want the media crawling all over the place! My clinic is meant to give comfort and practical advice to women who've been hurt and shocked, not sensational stuff for the tabloids.'

'Charlotte, it wasn't meant to be like that. I was trying to help—to give publicity to the cause.'

'Publicity isn't the answer, James. I don't need flashy celebrity stuff. I need people who are going to be able to give these women support and advocacy, counselling and information.

Which they're not going to get with a pack of journalists baying outside. You don't have a clue, do you? Right now, I'm doing the centre for one day a week, plus the website and a phone support one evening a week, but I want it to grow. It doesn't stand a chance if there's going to be photographers and journalists sniffing around for scandal.'

'Charlotte, listen—'

'No, *you* listen to me, James. Rape's the most under-reported crime in the country, for a good reason. Women who've been attacked feel dirty, feel as if it's their fault, when it isn't. They're scared nobody's going to believe them. Four out of five don't even go to the police—and even if they do go to the police, a quarter of those have left it more than a day and it's too late to…' She choked for a moment. 'Too late to collect the evidence. And the trials are a mockery. It's slowly getting better, but still so many jurors just think the woman's asking for it or making it up to get revenge on the bloke. And it's not like that. The majority of women know their attacker, but it doesn't mean they want to be forced into having sex.'

James looked horrified.

'Centres like mine help women—but now, instead of having a quiet place to come for help, they've got the press shining a spotlight over them.'

'This wasn't supposed to happen.'

'You've lived with the paparazzi all your life. You're used to them—and, if anything, you thrive on the attention. You can't help seeking it out. Yes, you worked hard organising the ball and you raised a lot of money for good causes—but you like to be *seen* raising the money,' Charlotte said bitterly. Because that was the truth of it. 'You want people to know what you've done, so you get public acknowledgement and have everyone talking about what a great guy you are.'

'It's not like that,' James protested.

'No? I told you I didn't want the nationals involved, and you didn't listen. You just went right on ahead with it.'

'I thought you were just being…well…shy.'

'Shy?' She stared at him in disbelief. 'It's got nothing to do with shyness and everything to do with wanting to keep my life private.' Her lip curled. 'You might be a brilliant doctor, but as a person I think you're a total and utter…' She dragged in a breath, then used a word that really shocked him, coming from her.

'I'll work with you simply because I have to and I don't want my patients to suffer,' she said, 'but that's as far as it goes. I don't want to see you any more than strictly necessary.'

And she walked away before he could say another word.

She wasn't finished yet. James was just the first one she wanted to talk to. Buoyed up with anger, she strode back out to the hospital entrance.

The moment she appeared, the cameras started snapping.

'Charlotte, Charlotte, give us a smile,' several called.

She held up one hand, extending her index finger, and the hubbub fell silent.

'You're blocking the entrance to the hospital and you're getting in the way of the patients and the staff. That's not fair.' She took a deep breath. 'Come with me and I'll talk to you.'

There were calls of 'Good girl' and 'That's right, darlin'!'

But, to her relief, they moved away from the hospital entrance.

'Please listen to me,' she said quietly. 'There isn't a story for you here. I'm not sleeping with James Alexander and I have no intention of seeing him outside work. He's my colleague. I work with him—and I worked with him on the dance evening to raise money for the hospital.'

'Bet that's not all that was raised, darlin',' one of them called.

Charlotte took a deep breath. Willed herself to stay calm in front of the crudeness. 'This is a hospital. I'm a doctor. So is James. We work with sick children. And that's all there is to it.'

When the questions continued, she realised just how naïve she'd been. They didn't want the truth: they wanted to sell newspapers.

Again, she held her hand up. 'If you want a real story…'

They fell silent, agog—clearly believing that she was going to spill some scandal. Well, she wasn't. She was going to try and make the best of a bad job. 'What I suggest you do is talk to the hospital's press department. With my patients' permission, I'm happy for any of you to sit in my clinic, one at a time. You can talk to my patients and their parents, and you'll hear the stories of children overcoming real odds—children who'd die if people like me weren't around to do something to help them. Children who'd die if people didn't fill out donor cards or give blood. That's the real story here. Courage and kindness making the world go round. *Other* people, not me.'

'What about James?' someone called.

She sighed. 'I already told you. I'm here to do my job and so is Mr Alexander. To save children's lives. Will you let us do that?'

There was no comment, though she thought she could see shame flushing several faces.

'And I hope,' she said softly, 'that any money you've made from pictures and untrue stories of last night, you'll do the decent thing and give it to someone who needs it more. Make something good happen out of all this mess. Now, excuse me. I've got patients to see.'

And then she walked back in to the hospital, her head held high.

But the pep talk didn't work. Or maybe the paparazzi just didn't care, Charlotte thought, because they were still chasing her. Doorstepping her over the whole weekend.

By Tuesday, she knew that she couldn't do her normal stint at the centre. Couldn't drag the press with her to Penhally, besieging her uncle's surgery and bringing media attention to women who needed support, not scandal-mongering. The only way she could protect the centre was to close it for the day. And her anger with James grew minute by minute; he'd put her in an impossible position. She barely spoke to him at work; she just about managed to put their joint patients first and maintain a professional attitude, but rebuffed every offer of lunch or a coffee. She was only glad that he hadn't tried some over-the-top gesture like sending her roses—or she would probably have ended up throwing them at him.

And she found it very hard to be polite when the parents of patients she saw for follow-up appointments asked about James or mentioned seeing them in the paper.

The worst was Judy Martyn, when Ellis came back for a check-up.

'You looked so lovely together in the newspapers,' Judy said. 'The perfect couple. I should've guessed, the way you worked together—such a perfect team.'

If only Judy knew how far they were from being a team. And perfect didn't even begin to come into the equation where James was concerned.

'We're just colleagues,' Charlotte replied, trying very hard to smile when she really wanted to scream. 'Really, I barely know him.'

And as for the man she'd been falling in love with…

Well, he didn't exist.

On Thursday, she had a polite call from the surgical team's secretary, asking to set up an appointment to see Millie Fowler's parents with James.

Ha. A week ago, James would've dropped in to see her before clinic or surgery and synchronised his schedule with hers. And although part of her missed that easiness between them, a larger part of her was relieved that he was doing things formally. It meant he was respecting what she'd said.

All the same, she felt sick with nerves when it got to two

o'clock, knowing that she'd have to face James and work as a team with him. There was no alternative. She could hardly refuse to see her patients, and switching caseloads with Tim would be unfair to all their patients as well as to Tim.

James arrived at the special care baby unit at exactly the same time she did.

'Dr Walker,' he said coolly.

'Mr Alexander.' She, too, could do cool and formal. Even though being close to him again made all her insides ache.

Together—and yet as far apart as they could possibly be— they walked into the room where Millie was lying in a crib, having oxygen therapy.

'Mr and Mrs Fowler? I'm James Alexander, the surgeon, and this is Charlotte Walker, the cardiologist,' James introduced them both.

Gently, Charlotte took them through the diagnosis. 'Millie has a heart condition known as tetralogy of Fallot. It sounds scary, but it's the most common heart condition and plenty of babies go on to do really well.'

'Dr Cook said that she had a heart murmur,' Mrs Fowler said. 'And that she was a blue baby.'

Charlotte nodded. 'I've run some tests, as you know, so I could take a closer look at Millie's heart and what's going on. There are four parts to her condition.' Putting as much as she could into layman's terms, she explained the condition to Millie's parents: a narrowed pulmonary valve which obstructed the blood flow, a hole in the ventricle and an enlarged aortic valve which allowed unoxygenated blood to circulate through the boy; and a thickened muscular wall to Millie's right ventricle because it had to pump blood at a higher pressure.

'She will need surgery,' James said, 'where I'll close the hole in her heart so the blood can flow normally again, but that won't be until she's six months old.'

'So does she have to stay in hospital until after the surgery?' Mr Fowler asked.

'No, you'll be able to take her home,' Charlotte reassured her. 'But you might find she has "tetralogy spells" where she'll be a bit irritable and she'll look blue. That's because there isn't enough oxygen in her blood—the blood's darker and looks blue, and you'll notice it more in her lips and fingertips. Sometimes just lifting her knees up gently, like this…' she demonstrated '…will help, and give her a cuddle.'

'But if she has a lot of these spells, we might need to take her in for an operation called a BT shunt, to make sure Millie gets enough blood flow to her lungs. I'll be able to remove the shunt when she has the operation at six months,' James explained.

'It's a lot to take in,' Charlotte said, 'so I've got some leaflets for you. You're bound to have questions afterwards, so I'll come in again and see you and Millie tomorrow, and we can talk over anything you're worried about or want to know more about.'

'Thank you.' Mrs Fowler looked worried sick.

Charlotte reached over and squeezed her hand. 'I know it's worrying,' she said softly, 'and you're probably feeling a bit overwhelmed right now, but things will get better. Millie's in really good hands, and we can put you in touch with other parents who've been through exactly this and can help support you. Obviously we're here and you can talk to us as any time, but it does help to talk to other parents.'

Mrs Fowler nodded, clearly too choked to talk.

Charlotte gently said goodbye. James clearly intended leaving the ward with her, but she managed to avoid him by the simple strategy of going to the loo.

Ah, hell. She'd been through worse—much worse—in Liverpool. Things would settle down again. It would just take time. And until then…she just needed to keep her distance from James. To stop thinking about him and wishing that things had been different.

CHAPTER ELEVEN

KATE was asleep on the sofa; gently, Rob covered her with a blanket, and went to remind the boys to be quiet while they finished their homework as Kate was sleeping.

But he couldn't resist peeking in at her before heading for the kitchen.

When Annette had been killed, the bottom had dropped out of his world. He'd never thought he'd fall in love again. And then Kate had arrived in his life, sweet and warm and one of life's fixers. The more he'd got to know her, the more he'd liked her—and when he'd finally plucked up the courage to ask her out, he'd been amazed that she'd actually said yes.

Liking had turned to love. And he knew without a doubt that he wanted to marry Kate. Part of him wanted to wake her up and ask her there and then. Ask her to make him the happiest man alive.

But it really wouldn't be fair to ask her.

Not now, when she was so vulnerable. Near the tail end of her treatment, but still with the shadow of cancer hanging over her. Knowing Kate, she'd refuse—not because she didn't care about him but because she wouldn't want him to run the risk of becoming a widower for the second time.

It was a risk he was more than prepared to run, but he'd wait. Until Kate had had a chance to recover from the radiotherapy, go to her three-month check-up and get the all-clear. When she'd be in a place to meet him as his equal, in her eyes.

'And then, Kate Althorp,' he said very softly in the living-room doorway, 'I'm going to ask you to do me the greatest honour. I'm going to ask you to let me love you for the rest of our lives. I'm going to ask you to marry me.'

The weekend was the most miserable that James could ever remember. The end of a whole week where he'd ached with missing Charlotte. And it scared him to find how much he missed her. He'd never, ever felt like this before.

And then it hit him with a shock.

He loved her.

Really loved her.

Though she certainly wasn't ready to hear those words from him. She might never be. He was going to have to work really hard to establish the old easiness between them—and, given the way she'd been with him at work for the last week, he was beginning to wonder if he ever would be able to do it.

How had it become such a mess? He'd meant to use his celebrity connections for a good reason, to draw attention to what Charlotte was doing and how important the work was. The idea had been to raise the profile of the clinic and get more people to donate funds. And he'd got it wrong. Big time.

This was worse than when he'd discovered the pictures of Sophia draped over the Italian on his father's yacht—worse than when he'd realised his marriage was an utter sham and Sophia hadn't loved him for himself at all.

But it wasn't himself he felt bad for, it was Charlotte. He hated himself for hurting her and causing her problems with the centre. It was so important to her—and, thanks to his interference, he'd heard that she hadn't been able to avoid the paparazzi and work at the centre that week.

He couldn't get her accusation out of his head: that he did good, but wanted to make sure that everyone saw him doing it.

He'd never thought of it that way, but he was beginning to realise that she had a point. He did lead a flashy lifestyle, and the celebrity world he moved in was incredibly shallow.

He'd considered sending her flowers to apologise but, apart from the fact that it wasn't anywhere near good enough, he was pretty sure she wouldn't accept them. The only way he could think of to start making amends was to give some quiet support to the cause that was obviously close to her heart.

And to write her a very, very personal letter of apology.

He just hoped she'd read it.

On Monday evening, Charlotte came home to find a hand-delivered envelope on her doormat. The address was typed. Junk mail, she thought, and opened it, ready to shred anything with her personal details and put the rest in the recycling bin.

But it contained two more envelopes. Both very good quality papers. And both were addressed in handwriting she recognised.

James's.

One said *Open me first* and the other *Open me second.*

She wasn't interested in anything he had to say. She really ought to just give them back to him, unopened. But then curiosity got the better of her and she read them.

The first one was a letter.

Hand-written. In fountain-pen, of course—James wouldn't use a cheap and cheerful ballpen.

But he'd clearly spent time over it. He hadn't typed it or sent an email. This was personal. And when she read it, she realised he was being sincere. Really laying himself open.

I'm so sorry about all the mess in the papers. I can't change the past but, if I could, I'd go back and do things differently.

Yeah. So would she.

I can't use my training to support your work at the centre,
because I realised that women who come to you for help
will probably want to see a female doctor. But if there's
anything else I can do, whether if it's licking stamps and
sticking them on envelopes, or delivering flyers by hand,
or cleaning the clinic and helping you lock up at the end
of a session, just tell me and I'll do it.

She smiled wryly. Hotshot surgeon James, licking stamps
and wielding a feather duster? Surreal. Though she knew he
meant it.

There's a cheque in the other envelope. I'm not trying to
be flash or buy you off, it's just the only thing I know how
to do. And it will buy you training for volunteers. I hope
that will go some way to making up the time you've
missed this week.

Quickly, she ripped open the second envelope. There was a
cheque, written out to the centre. She blinked at the size of it:
this really would make a difference.

It was probably small change to a man like James, a man
from such a wealthy background.

Then again, he'd been under no obligation to do this.

She turned back to the letter.

I miss you more than I ever thought was possible. There's
a big hole in my life shaped like you, and I don't know
how to begin to fill it because nobody else will do.

There was a lump in her throat as she read on.

But I understand that you want me to stay away, and I'll
respect your wishes. I hope you find happiness in the
future; I just wish it could have been with me.

She dragged in a breath and Pandora leaped onto her lap, purring.

'He misses me, Pandora.' And, if she was honest with herself, she missed him.

Pandora purred, as if saying that she did, too.

'And he sent me the cheque privately. He didn't have an art department mock up a gigantic cheque on featherboard and get the press there to take photographs and splash the story about. So he must have listened to what I said. He's trying to show me that he can do something good without being flashy.' She bit her lip. 'I was a bit hard on him.' Because she'd been so angry. And because she hadn't been honest with him before the ball, told him exactly why she didn't want publicity, he wouldn't have a clue why she was so angry. 'I think I owe him an explanation.'

The cat purred her agreement.

'I could ring him…but I think this is the kind of conversation I need to have face to face with him.' She paused. 'I'm sorry for deserting you again this evening, but I really ought to go and see him.'

Pandora simply rubbed against her and jumped off her lap, as if saying that she understood.

Charlotte checked the cat's water dish and put some extra biscuits in Pandora's food bowl.

When she opened the front door, to her relief, the paparazzi were nowhere to be seen. All the same, she took a circuitous route when she drove over to the waterside development where James lived.

Her heart was beating so hard as she walked up the steps to his front door, she was sure people must be able to hear it. Taking a deep breath, she rang the bell. Hopefully James was in—and would answer.

James thought about ignoring the doorbell—he wasn't expecting anyone and he wasn't in the mood for visitors—but then it rang again. Clearly whoever was out there wasn't going to give up.

When he opened the front door, he blinked several times, trying to clear his vision. But when he looked again she was still there.

'Charlotte?'

'May I come in?' she asked quietly.

'Sure.'

She waited until he'd closed the door behind them. 'I got your letter. And the cheque.'

'Good.'

'Thank you.'

'Pleasure.'

'And I owe you an apology.' She took a deep breath. 'Look, I know I've given you a hard time this week. I guess I over-reacted.'

He shrugged. 'Yes and no. You had a point—I do thrive on the attention of the press, probably because I've always been used to it. I never realised how intrusive it could be.'

'It wasn't just that.' She bit her lip. 'I didn't want the press dragging up stuff about me.'

'Stuff?'

'About my past.'

James had a nasty feeling that he knew what she was going to tell him, and he didn't want to hear it. He hated the idea that someone had hurt her. 'Charlotte, you don't have to confide in me.'

'Actually, I do. I should've trusted you before. Because then you'd have understood why I didn't want the national press there. I wasn't being shy, James. I don't want everyone at the hospital to stop seeing me as I am.'

He frowned. 'I'm not with you. Why would they do that?'

'It's messy.' She swallowed. 'And I don't usually talk about it.'

'I'd pretty much worked out that something had happened

to you,' James said quietly. 'So you don't have to tell me. It's why you were so wary of me when you first met me, and why you set up the centre. I can understand that.' He sighed. 'And I was so busy trying to do something to support you, I blocked out the fact that any publicity might pick up on your past and use it to hurt you.'

'I told Steffie it happened to someone else.' She bit her lip. 'Which it did. I was a different person then.'

'Of course that kind of experience would change you.' He raked a hand through his hair, uncomfortable with the discussion and not wanting to drag up memories that hurt her. 'Look, do you want a coffee or something?'

She shook her head. 'But I do need to be honest with you. I, um, haven't dated since…' She hesitated, as if she couldn't bear to speak the words. 'You were the first man I kissed,' she said eventually. 'The first man I even considered sleeping with.'

'And I let you down.'

She grimaced. 'You weren't in possession of all the facts.'

It was a more generous assessment than he felt he deserved.

'If I'd trusted you with the truth about me, would you have involved the nationals?' she asked.

He knew she was expecting him to say no. But she was being honest with him. He needed to be equally as straight with her. 'Actually, I probably would,' he said. 'But I would've handled it differently. We would've stayed in the background, as the organisers. And I would've talked to you properly about it beforehand, asked you if you wanted me to mention anything about the centre.'

'You would have listened to me?'

'Yes. And I'm sorry for not listening before, for assuming that you were just hiding your light under a bushel and carrying on regardless.'

She swallowed hard. 'That's what Michael did.'

'Michael?' The use of the name shocked him. 'You *knew* the guy?'

'Most vict—' She stopped short, shaking her head viciously. 'No. I'm *not* a victim. I'm not going to let him make me think that way about myself. But, yeah, most people know their attackers.' She dragged in a breath. 'We'd dated a couple of times. I thought he was a nice guy. Charming, good-looking.'

James really didn't like where this was heading. Terms that people had used about him, too.

'Then one night we went out dancing.'

Just what he'd made her do. Dance with him. In front of a crowd. He loved the glittery, sparkly events and he'd thought she'd find them as much fun as he did. Yet, all the time, he'd been twisting the knife—and Charlotte had been fighting the bad memories in private.

'He took me home, and I thought he was just going to kiss me goodnight and leave, but he started pushing me. I said no and he...' She shuddered and wrapped her arms round herself. 'He didn't listen. And he was bigger than I was. I couldn't fight him off.'

James didn't know what to say. Or do. He'd never been in a situation like this, and he really didn't want to make things harder for her. He'd already hurt her enough. The only thing he could do was act on his instincts and be honest, so he closed the gap between them and put his arms round her. 'I know this is probably inappropriate. But I don't know what to say or do,' he said. 'Other than that I want to beat him to a pulp for hurting you, and I want to hold you and protect you and make sure nobody ever hurts you again.'

'I don't need to be wrapped up in cotton wool. I just want to be treated decently.'

'I hope you know that I'd never...' He searched frantically for the right words, not wanting to make the situation harder for her.

'I know you wouldn't.' Her voice shuddered. 'But I never talk about it because I don't want people to look at me in pity. Or to whisper and wonder if I led him on.'

He pulled back just far enough for her to be able to see his eyes—to know that he was telling her the truth. 'I don't pity you and I know that you didn't lead him on. Nobody who knows you would ever pity you or make insinuations—sympathise, yes, but not look down on you.' He dragged in a breath. 'I'm sorry that you had to go through something so horrible, and I hate the thought of anyone treating you like that. But I admire the way you've held it together—and my guess is that anyone who works with you would see things the way I do. They'll be on your side.'

'I wasn't very together at the time,' she admitted. 'I felt so grubby. So disgusting.'

'You're *not* disgusting. You're brave and you're beautiful,' he said. 'So you told the police?'

She nodded. 'And I waived my right to anonymity. So it was in the papers.'

And she'd done that, knowing that the gutter press would try to dig up scandal? 'I take back what I said about brave. More like superhumanly courageous.'

'I just wanted to stop him doing it to anyone else,' she said simply. 'And the only way to do that, to get him the help he needed, was to…' Her breath hitched. 'I was so desperate for a shower. But I knew if I did, I'd get rid of the…of the evidence.'

He drew her closer. 'You don't have to tell me anything more.'

She was shivering. 'I do. I need this to be in the open, or we're not going to be able to move on from here. And I want to move on, James. I need to get past this. To go on with the rest of my life.'

With him?

He really, really hoped so.

'It took me a while to call the police. I was shaking so hard I couldn't dial the number. They came straight out, and they…they examined me. Questioned me.' She shuddered. 'I was lucky, because they believed me. One thing about having fair skin, you bruise easily.'

'The *bastard*,' James said, feeling his fists clench involuntarily. And he really, really wanted to give the guy back every single bruise he'd given Charlotte. With interest.

'He needed help. People don't behave like that unless they're really damaged.'

'You've got a more generous spirit than I have. I'd want the guy locked up and the key thrown away.'

'I wanted that, too,' she admitted. 'I'm only human. But I've had counselling, and I'm in a place now where I can help others. And that's why I wanted to set up the crisis centre. Because I've been there. I've come out the other side, and I want to help other people come out the other side, too.'

'I understand that now. And I really admire you for doing it. Doesn't it bring it all back to you, when you talk to women who've been in your situation?'

'Sort of, but it's slowly losing its power to hurt me.' She rested her forehead against his chest. 'There's still part of me that feels unclean. Even though I scrubbed my skin until it bled after the police had been. And that's why I don't date.'

He pressed a kiss on the top of her head. 'You're not unclean. You're strong and you're brave and you're gorgeous. And I'm humbled that you've trusted me with this. I'm not going to mention it to anyone—not because I pity you or think you led the guy on,' he added, just to underline the point, 'but because I respect your right to privacy. And if I'd had any idea, I would never, ever have put you in a situation like this.'

'I've been reading the papers every day. Just waiting for them to…to put two and two together and bring it all up again.'

And, unlike him, she hadn't grown up with media attention. Being its focus, like this, must be hell for her. 'If it makes you feel any better, according to *Great!* magazine, you wouldn't have sex with me if I was the last man on earth. They're enjoying playing with that far too much to spend time digging up any dirt on you.'

She pulled back to look him in the eye. 'So they're being nasty about you?'

He gave a half-shrug. 'They've done it before. I'll live.' She didn't need to know that they'd run pictures of Sophia draped over various European hunks, all of whom she'd found preferable to him during their marriage. 'They'll have photos of someone else next week—someone who drank too much at a party or was a bit indiscreet on the beach—and that will be the new story. Everyone will forget about us.'

'I hope so.' She bit her lip. 'It's horrible when the whole hospital's talking about you.'

He remembered people poring over the gossip magazines to get the next installment of the disaster of his marriage, the guilt on their faces and the way they'd hidden the magazines quickly when he'd walked into the room. The way that everywhere would go silent, and he'd known that they'd been discussing the mess of his so-called private life.

And no doubt it had been even worse for her. He at least was used to publicity and people talking about his family, whereas Charlotte was much more private. Professional, smiley—and kept her personal life completely under wraps. 'Yeah. I know,' he said softly, stroking her hair back from her forehead. 'And I'm sorry I've made it worse for you.'

'You didn't do it on purpose.'

'No. And I'd give a lot to be able to turn back time and change things.' He paused. 'But one thing I wouldn't change is coming to Cornwall. Meeting you.' He cupped her face briefly. 'You're the best thing that's ever happened to me. And I know I let you down, but if you give me the chance I'd like to make it up to you.'

'That letter…you really meant it, didn't you?'

He nodded. 'It went through quite a few drafts. Even that

one sounded wrong. As if I was trying to be smooth and smarm my way out of things. I know you think I'm flashy—'

'You *are* flashy,' she cut in dryly. 'I bet you used an expensive fountain pen.'

'Yes, and it was a twenty-first present from my grandmother.' He smiled ruefully. 'I don't know if I can change all the glitzy stuff. But, for you, I'll try.'

'A new start.'

He nodded. 'Look...I know this is going to sound completely inappropriate, but it's not how I mean it. Have you eaten yet tonight?'

'No.'

'Neither have I. There's salad in the fridge. How about I order a pizza to be delivered? Nothing flashy. Just you and me, spending a little time together.'

'I'd like that,' she said, and her smile made him feel warm for the first time in days.

She opted for mineral water rather than wine—seeing as she'd be driving back to her place later—and James was chopping vegetables for the salad when the doorbell went.

'Do you want me to get that?' she asked.

'If you don't mind. I paid by credit card, so you don't have to worry about paying.'

Charlotte walked downstairs, opened the front door—and slammed it again in horror. Because it wasn't the pizza delivery boy—there was a sea of paparazzi. Cameras flashing, people all talking at once at top volume and thrusting microphones towards her.

James must have heard the door slam, because he came straight down into the hall. 'What's the matter?'

'Press.'

He groaned. 'Charlotte, I'm so sorry. I have no idea how they knew you were here.'

'Maybe one of them was outside when I arrived, and I didn't notice.'

'They'll have staked out the back, too.'

'Then how am I going to get home?'

He sighed. 'I think we're just going to have to wait them out.'

'I…Are you suggesting I stay the night?' Panic skittered through her. Yes, she was attracted to him—but she wasn't sure that she was ready to skip a few steps and stay overnight at his place.

He took her hand. 'Look at me, Charlotte.'

She did so.

'I promise you, I won't do anything you're uncomfortable with. I'm attracted to you and I want to—well, court you, I suppose. So I'm not going to take advantage of the situation. We'll take things at your pace.'

The doorbell went again. 'I'll deal with this. Go into the kitchen and close the door,' James directed. 'They won't hassle you there.'

She headed for the kitchen, and he appeared a few minutes later carrying a box. 'Pizza,' he said with a smile.

'James, I'm sorry, but I'm not sure I could eat anything now.' She closed her eyes. 'Telling you as much as I did about my past, and now this…I'm not hungry any more.'

'Trust me, the carbs will make you feel better. If you let your blood sugar dip, you'll feel even worse.' He dished up. 'Help yourself to salad.'

She forced herself to take a couple of mouthfuls, to be polite. And, to her surprise, he was right. It did make her feel better.

When they'd finished, he said quietly, 'What I suggest we do now is sit down, listen to some music, and just ignore whatever's outside. They can't get in, they can't see into my living room—and eventually they'll realise they don't have a story and they'll go away.'

She let him lead her into his living room, and made no protest when he settled her on his lap, holding her close. Despite knowing what was outside, she felt safe here with James, and finally the stresses of the last week caught up with her and she fell asleep.

James had noticed the dark shadows under Charlotte's eyes. No doubt she'd slept as badly as he had, the last few days. He could always carry her down the stairs to his bed—but he very much doubted she'd continue sleeping through it. She wasn't a toddler. And if she woke while he were carrying her off, given her traumatic past…No, there was only one thing for it.

'Charlotte,' he said softly, stroking her cheek.

She murmured, and snuggled closer.

'Much as I would love to stay here like this,' he said, 'we'll both get a crick in our necks. The press isn't going away just yet, so why don't you grab a couple of hours' sleep on my bed?'

Her eyelids snapped open at that. 'Your bed.'

'I'll sleep in the spare room,' he said. 'But my bed's more comfortable, which is why I'm offering it to you.'

'I…'

'I'll stay with you until you fall asleep again,' he said. 'You'll be safe. It'll be fine.'

She shivered. 'If you're sure.'

'I'm sure.' He brushed his lips against her cheek. 'I did think about carrying you downstairs, but it's a bit too macho. Even for someone with an ego the size of Mars.'

'I apologised for that, a long time ago.'

He laughed. 'I know. I'm just teasing. Come on.' He gently urged her to her feet, then led her downstairs to his room. He pulled the duvet back for her.

'James, I…'

'It'll be more comfortable. And I'm staying above the quilt, OK? Just a nap. And we'll escape the press in a few hours' time.'

'Thank you,' she said quietly.

He settled the duvet round her, then lay next to her. Although he desperately wanted to hold her close, he was going to take this slowly. At her pace. Right now, the most important thing was for Charlotte to feel safe. Protected. By him.

CHAPTER TWELVE

THE next morning, Charlotte was woken by an alarm—an alarm that definitely wasn't hers.

She opened her eyes with a jolt, instantly aware that she was still in James's bed. And at almost the same moment she realised that James was still lying beside her. His body was curled round hers and his arm was draped over her, holding her close. A more intimate position than she'd been in with anyone for years.

'Good morning,' James said softly.

The weight of his arm lifted from her, and a moment or two later the shrill of the alarm clock stopped.

'Good morning.' She swallowed hard and turned onto her back, preparing to face him.

'Are you all right?' he asked.

'Yes,' she fibbed.

As if he guessed that, actually, she was incredibly nervous, he said quietly, 'I'm sorry. I honestly meant to go to the spare room as soon as you went to sleep, then wake you at three and drive you home myself. Except...' He smiled ruefully. 'I fell asleep, too. Luckily my alarm's a twenty-four-hour one or we'd both be late for work.'

'You must be freezing.' The duvet was still between them, so he'd had no covers over him during the night.

'It wasn't that cold last night. I'm OK.' He dismissed it with a smile.

He'd spent the night with her. Slept beside her.

But he hadn't taken advantage of her.

James Alexander really was the man she'd hoped he was. A man who'd keep his word. A man she could trust.

Charlotte shifted to her side, and curved her palm along his jaw. 'Thank you.'

'Why?' he asked.

'For being honourable.'

'Not all men are like the one who...' He stopped, clearly not wanting to voice it, and hurt her.

'Date-raped me.' At his widened eyes, she said quietly, 'I've come to terms with it, James. I've had counselling. I can say the word without flinching. I won't forget it, and I'm afraid I can't forgive it either—but I'm also not going to let it ruin the rest of my life.'

'I'm glad of that. I'm only sorry that I've exposed you to gossip and speculation.'

'It can't be as bad as when it actually happened,' Charlotte said. 'As you told me last night, if I think about it rationally, the people I work with are my friends. They know me. They'll be on my side.'

'Surely your coll—' He stopped abruptly.

'Michael worked at the hospital, too, in the finance department. And he was a charmer. Everyone liked him. People took sides.' She closed her eyes. 'Walking into work the next day...I was convinced everyone would know. And that he'd come onto the ward, pretending that nothing had happened.'

James drew her closer. 'Did he?'

'No. The police arrested him. But I had to face him in court, months later.' She shivered. 'He said what he did wasn't that bad because we'd been out together a few times and it was the next step in our relationship. He said he'd just rushed me a bit—

and I wasn't a virgin, so it wasn't as if he'd done anything that bad.'

'Yes, he bloody well had!' James said. 'He didn't have the right to make you do anything. I want to beat the guy to a pulp.'

'Apart from the fact that you need your hands in working order in Theatre, I don't somehow think the prison warders will let you do that,' she said dryly.

'So the jury convicted him?'

She shivered. 'I remember going to the sentencing and my solicitor holding my hand. I was so scared they'd blame me and he'd be let off, even though other women had come forward anonymously—they hadn't spoken up beforehand because they didn't think anyone would believe them. They thought he'd say they were trying to get revenge on him for dumping them.'

'I…Charlotte, I don't know what to say. I can't understand how a man could…It's just…' He shook his head in apparent disbelief.

'He was damaged, too. I had to remind myself he needed help to stop. Just as I needed help to come to terms with what happened.' She moved closer, needing James's warmth. 'They gave him seven years. And when it was all over, I just felt drained. I remembered coming to Penhally when I was a kid, staying with Uncle Nick and Aunt Annabel. I loved Cornwall. There's something about the sea, something healing about the beaches here. So I rang Nick and asked if I could come and stay. He found me a flat and this job came up at St Piran's.'

'And everything was fine until I interfered.'

'You were trying to do what you thought was the right thing.'

'And it was the wrong thing. I know that now. And I'm truly sorry.' He stroked her hair. 'It's a lot to ask, but if you could find it in you to forgive me, make a fresh start?'

She nodded. 'I have to admit, I missed you, too. Even when I was angry with you.' She paused. 'Maybe we can have dinner tonight.'

'I'd like that. A lot.' He looked steadily at her. 'Though there's something I need you to be clear about. You know what I do for a living. If we agree a time and a place, I can't promise to be on time and I can't promise that I won't stand you up.'

Charlotte knew immediately what he meant, though she had no idea why he was making the point. She already knew the situation. He'd been late for several of their dance lessons for the same reason. 'If one of your patients develops complications, of course you're not going to leave someone else to deal with it.'

'Though I'll give you as much warning as I can if I can't make it or I'm going to be late.'

'That goes for me, too,' she reminded him. 'I might get called to the children's ward or the special baby care unit. It's part and parcel of what we do, James. And it's pretty obvious: if you want to date someone who works regular hours, you don't date a medic.'

'I'm glad we're clear on that.' He took her hand and lifted it to his lips. 'We need to get ready for work. I'm afraid I can't do much about clean clothes, though you're welcome to a pair of my jeans and a shirt, if you want them. My bathroom's through that door over there, and I'll find you a clean towel and a new toothbrush.'

'Thanks, but I'd rather shower and change at home.' She grimaced. 'I just hate the idea of having a shower and then having to put dirty clothes back on. But I'll say yes please to the toothbrush. Very gratefully.'

'I'll sort it now. How about some breakfast? Coffee?'

She shook her head. 'I need to get going.'

'Pandora?' he guessed.

'She'll be OK—I left her plenty of water and I fed her before I decided to come and see you. And the catflap works on her microchip, so letting her in and out isn't a problem.' She bit her lip. 'But are the paparazzi still going to be waiting out there?'

'They'll think,' James said, 'that I drove you home at stupid o'clock in the morning to avoid them.'

Which had been the original plan.

'They won't think I've stayed the night?'

'If they're anything like the ones who usually trail me, they know I don't let anyone stay the night,' he said dryly, 'so there's no point in staying until breakfast.'

It took her a while to digest that. So James didn't let anyone that close? What about his reputation as a man who dated more women than she'd had hot dinners?

She already knew the answer. Press exaggeration.

So the fact James had allowed her closer than he normally allowed people...that was definite food for thought.

When she emerged from the bathroom after washing her face and cleaning her teeth, he smiled at her. 'I've checked outside and the coast's clear.'

'Thanks. And, um, thanks for last night.'

'My pleasure. I'll see you at work.'

She drove home, showered and changed, and then walked to work. For the first time in more than a week she greeted everyone with a smile that reached her eyes. She actually caught herself singing in the corridor on the way to the children's ward. And she regretted that she hadn't suggested to James that he should sit in on her operation that morning, closing a hole in a three-year-old boy's heart using a balloon on the end of a catheter. Although the operation still involved a general anaesthetic, it meant that the little boy didn't need to have open-heart surgery involving having his heart stopped and being put on bypass, and he'd recover within a day and without scarring across his chest.

James caught up with her at lunchtime. 'Good morning?'

'ASD with a septal occluder in the cath lab,' she said. 'It worked, and little Barney's doing fine.'

'Next time you do one of those, I want to be nosy,' James said.

She smiled. 'Next time, I'll invite you along.'

'Good.' He did a swift check to make sure they wouldn't be overheard. 'Dinner tonight. Anywhere in particular you'd like me to book?'

'My place, and I'm cooking,' she said. 'Because then we can talk without worrying about who's listening in and how many cameras are around.'

'Fair point,' he said. 'Half-seven?'

'Perfect.'

As always, James was on time, and Charlotte answered the door very quickly.

'I don't think I was followed,' James said. 'I took the long way round, just in case. But I think we've finished being a nine days' wonder.'

'Good,' Charlotte said feelingly.

'I was going to bring you flowers, but was I was terrified of getting it wrong and making you think I was being flashy.'

'A small bunch of flowers,' Charlotte said with a grin, 'is perfectly acceptable. Just not a whole florist's.'

He handed her a carrier bag that contained two bottles of wine and some seriously good chocolate. 'I hope these are OK. I didn't know whether to bring red or white, so I brought both.'

And both were much posher than the wine she normally bought. She squeezed his hand. 'James, you're trying too hard—and you only needed to bring yourself. This is just supper, like you've had here before. Nothing that fussy. Come and sit down. Dinner will be about another ten minutes.'

The second that James was sitting on the sofa, Pandora leapt onto his lap, settled herself, and started purring.

'Given her background, I think I'm flattered,' James said, stroking the cat.

It was the most relaxed evening she'd spent with him since the evening before the ball, and it was only when she offered James another coffee that he looked at the clock. 'It's getting late. I really ought to be going—so, regretfully, I'd better say no to the coffee.'

She saw him to the door.

'Thank you for this evening. I really enjoyed it,' he said. His gaze dropped to her mouth, and then back to her eyes—as if asking permission.

'James,' she said softly. 'If you want to kiss me goodnight, then kiss me.'

'I want to. But I don't want to rush you, do anything you're uncomfortable with.'

She smiled wryly. 'Says the man who brought me *pain au chocolat* and then licked chocolate from my mouth. In my office. When anyone could've walked in.'

'If I'd known what had happened to you, I would never have pushed you like that.'

'So what's the difference now? You said that what I told you didn't change the way you saw me.'

'It hasn't. I still think you're incredibly gorgeous.'

'A week ago, you wouldn't have hesitated. So knowing about Michael *has* changed things.'

'In a way.' He looked serious. 'Charlotte, as long as you know that I'm listening to you—and if you say stop, I'll stop immediately—'

She smiled at him. 'James, just shut up and kiss me.'

She slid her hands behind his neck, drew his face down to hers, and brushed her mouth against his.

He responded instantly, letting her deepen the kiss and wrapping his arms round her so she was left in no doubt of his physical arousal yet at the same time keeping his tough light and unthreatening.

When the kiss finally ended, he asked softly, 'OK?'

'Very OK.'

'Good.' He touched his mouth briefly to hers. 'Sleep well. I'll see you tomorrow.'

Over the next few days, Charlotte and James spent more time together outside work—to the point where it was as if the ball had never happened. Somehow they'd managed to recapture their old easiness, even though Charlotte was very aware that James was being careful with her and just the tiniest bit over-protective.

At the weekend, they explored the local coast and found a quiet, practically deserted beach; as they walked along the shoreline, barefooted and holding hands, James finally opened up to her.

'Before you, my life was a mess,' he said. 'I really crashed and burned with Sophia.'

Sensing that he needed to tell her, the way she'd told him about what had happened with Michael, she just squeezed his hand and listened.

'She was part of my crowd. My family knew hers, and I guess I thought she was my type.' He smiled wryly. 'Tall, slender and beautiful, with this cloud of dark hair. On paper we were suited, with similar backgrounds and what have you.'

Charlotte could hear the 'but', and voiced it.

He sighed. 'I'm a doctor. Yes, I've chosen a flashy specialty and I love the challenges of my job—but I do it because I want to make people better. I want to make a difference to people's lives. And that's what Sophia couldn't understand—that my patients come before my social life and always will. She wanted me to have a clinic in Harley Street and work nine to five.' He grimaced. 'Actually, I think she wanted me to change special-ties. Go into plastics, like your cousin Jack.'

'And that's not what you wanted?'

'No. If I had gone into plastics, I would've wanted to do what he did. Specialise in burns. I mean, of course there are good reasons why people need cosmetic surgery. The boy who gets bullied at school because his ears stick out, so he wants them pinned back to make him less of a target; the girl who's so self-conscious about her nose that she can't bring herself to date or believe that someone would want her. Sure.' He sighed. 'Though even then I'd say one of the talking treatments would help more, because a few surface changes aren't going to be enough to repair psychological damage. But Sophia wasn't thinking about that sort of plastics. She was thinking more along the lines of face lifts and botox—I think she liked the idea of me being plastic surgeon to the celebs, and then she could add my patients to her social circle.'

'Ouch.'

He shrugged. 'If I was late for a party or something—and I admit, I often was—she'd flounce off and hit the shops until she'd spent her way out of a bad mood, or she'd fly off somewhere for a few days to chill out. With Dad owning the hotel chain, she was assured of the best suites in the best hotels in the most fashionable cities.'

Privately, Charlotte felt that James's ex sounded as if she needed to grow up.

'Marrying her was the biggest mistake of my life. I think I knew that even on our wedding day. It was a bit on the glitzy side, even for me. Her wedding dress was more catwalk than bride, and...' he grimaced '...although she insisted on tight security and had a hissy fit when unofficial pictures appeared in the gossip magazines, I think she enjoyed all the attention.'

Attention that Charlotte most definitely didn't.

'But I wasn't the husband she needed. I put my job before her, and I didn't try hard enough to make the marriage work,' James said.

'It takes two to make a marriage,' Charlotte reminded him softly.

'But it wasn't all her fault. I didn't meet her expectations. And she decided that if I wasn't going to give her the attention she wanted, she'd find it elsewhere.' He sighed. 'The first thing I knew about it was when I saw the pictures in *Great!* magazine. Topless, on my father's yacht, draped over an up-and-coming Italian model. The exposure...' he gave a wry smile at the pun '...was good for his career. And it did me a favour, really. It made me realise that this wasn't how I wanted to live, and something had to change.'

'So you got divorced?'

'That was the problem, You have to be married for a year before you can be divorced.'

'How long had you been married?' she asked gently.

'Six months.' He blew out a breath. 'I had to wait it out and try to ignore the men she flaunted in the gossip rags. And I swore I'd never get involved with anyone again.'

She regarded their joined hands. 'Hmm. Not involved.'

'You're different,' he said. 'I knew you were different, the first moment I met you. And the more I get to know you, the more I realise…' He stopped.

'Realise what?'

He shook his head. 'Later. Anyway, thanks for listening.'

'No problem. And thank you for trusting me. It goes without saying that I'm not going to betray your confidence.'

He gave a half-shrug. 'I think you've taught me how to trust. You opened up to me first. Made yourself vulnerable. So I feel safe with you.'

She tightened her fingers round his. 'I feel safe with you, too,' she whispered.

On Wednesday, while Charlotte was working at the surgery, Nick dropped in to see her at lunchtime. 'How's it going?' he asked.

'Really good.' She smiled at him. 'I'm helping people, Nick—and it's helping me leave the past behind.'

'Uh-huh.'

She looked at him and frowned. 'You've got shadows under your eyes. Do you want to go out for a sandwich or something?'

'I'm fine. Just…things on my mind,' Nick hedged.

'You know,' Charlotte said quietly, 'Annabel would be furious with you for letting yourself be unhappy like this. Whatever's eating at you, Nick, maybe it's time to let it go. I've done that myself, and it's incredible how much better it made me feel.'

Nick wasn't sure whether anything could make him feel better. Or how he could let the past go. He'd betrayed Annabel with his first love, on one of the darkest nights of his life. And he'd gone on to make Kate miserable by refusing to recognise who Jem really was—though how could he do that without risking his newly fixed relationship with his grown-up children?

As for Kate herself… Guilt ripped at him. He hadn't exactly been supportive during her illness, had he? True, she'd pushed him away. But every time he'd tried, he'd seen Rob there. Looking tenderly at her. Being there for her. Hell, the man was even *living* with Kate now. Nick had seen them on the beach together—Kate, Jem, Rob and Matt—and they looked like a proper family.

He ought to just leave her be. Let her go and have her chance of happiness with Rob.

And yet…

'Nick?' Charlotte said softly. 'If you want an ear—someone who won't judge you or argue or push you—you know where I am.'

'I do. Thank you.' He forced a smile to her face. 'Well, I'd better let you get on.'

'Sure you don't fancy lunch at the Smugglers'?' Charlotte asked.

'Thanks, but I'll pass.' He paused. 'James…he's being all right to you? Not pushing you?'

'He's fine.' Charlotte's smile was full of tenderness. Of love. And Nick was pretty sure where her relationship was going.

The same way that everyone else's seemed to.

Except his own.

The first Saturday in October, Charlotte rang James. 'Are you busy?'

'Not particularly. Why?'

'There's something I want to show you. I'll come and pick you up.'

'Why don't I come and pick you up?' he asked.

'Because it's a surprise, and I want to drive.'

'You could always drive the Aston,' he suggested.

'Really?'

'I put your name on the insurance. So if you want to…'

'Oh, yes!'

He laughed. 'You sound like a kid in a sweetshop. I'm on my way now.'

When he rang the doorbell and handed her the keys to the Aston Martin, Charlotte beamed at him. She drove immensely carefully at first, and James teased, 'You're allowed to go up to the speed limit, you know.'

'Very funny.' But she relaxed after that, and seemed to be enjoying handling the car as much as he did. And he loved seeing the sheer pleasure on her face.

Pleasure he'd like to see there for another reason.

But he'd keep himself in check until she was ready.

'So where are we going?' he asked.

'There and back, to see how far it is.'

'What?'

'That's what my parents always used to tell me,' she said. 'Funnily enough, they used to say it on this very stretch of road.'

James recognised the route to Penhally. 'We're going to see Jack? Your uncle?'

'Neither.' She parked outside a large, slightly ramshackle house. 'We're going to see some friends of mine.'

A very pretty woman with golden hair opened the door and greeted Charlotte with a hug. 'Charlotte, *cara,* it's lovely to see you—and you won't believe how much they've grown!'

Grown? James was completely lost. Who or what had grown?

'James, this is Melinda Lovak—she's the one who rescued

Pandora and introduced her to me,' Charlotte said. 'Melinda, this is James Alexander.'

'Pleased to meet you,' James said politely. And then he frowned. 'Don't I know you from somewhere?'

Melinda rolled her eyes. 'Probably the same place as I know you. *Great!* magazine.'

It suddenly clicked. 'Princess Melinda Fortescue.' The heiress to the principality of Contarini.

'Mrs Melinda Lovak nowadays,' she corrected with a warm smile. 'Lovely to meet you too, James. Come in. Dragan and Alessandro are out in the garden.'

Charlotte took his hand and they followed Melinda through the huge old-fashioned kitchen to the garden.

There, in the middle of the lawn, a toddler sat next to a black flatcoat retriever, and climbing all over both of them were six puppies, three black and three brown. A tall, dark-haired man was chatting to the little boy; he looked up as Melinda, Charlotte and James joined them.

Charlotte introduced them quickly. 'Dragan, this is James. James, this is Dragan and Alessandro.'

Dragan and James gave each other a slightly wary nod.

Charlotte exclaimed in delight at the pups. 'Look at them—I can't believe how huge they're getting! Dare I ask why they have little bits of wool round their necks?'

'So we can tell them apart,' Dragan explained. 'The wool's really soft, so it doesn't hurt them; it breaks easily if they chew it or get it caught on something, and we can replace it as the pups grow.'

'So I assume this one's a girl.' Charlotte knelt down and scooped up a black puppy with a bright pink thread around its neck.

'Er, no. Alessandro chose the colours,' Melinda said, smiling. 'That one's a boy.'

James just stared, utterly enchanted. Especially when the pup promptly licked Charlotte's face and she laughed.

'They're gorgeous,' James breathed, including Charlotte in the description.

'Aren't they just?' Dragan stroked the dog's head. 'My Bramble's done really well.'

'I'm horribly envious,' James confessed. A houseful of puppies. Something he'd desperately wanted as a child, but there had never been time.

'Pick one up and have a cuddle,' Melinda said. 'We need to socialise them. The more people they meet and have a fuss with, the better.'

James needed no second invitation. 'When I was a kid, I always wanted a black dog called Dylan who'd go everywhere with me.'

'I had a dog like that when I was a boy,' Dragan said, 'and now I have Bramble.'

'Bam-bam,' Alessandro said, beaming and stroking the dog. 'Zando loves Bam-bam.' He grinned at them, clearly pleased with himself. 'Look, puppies!'

'"Dog" was his second word,' Melinda said dryly. '"Dada", of course, being the first.'

What would it be like to have a little boy looking up to you, calling you Dada? James wondered, and settled himself on the lawn next to the little boy. How much he'd like something like this in the future. To live in an old rambling place, instead of a gleaming modern townhouse that looked as if it belonged in a photo shoot and was definitely a house rather than a home. He could imagine coming home at the end of a hard day to his children and puppies and someone he loved so much he'd walk to the end of the world and back for her—someone who'd feel that same way about him.

His gaze connected with Charlotte's, and he had to look away, not wanting her to see the longing in his soul and be scared off.

Because he knew exactly who that person was, the one for whom he'd walk to the end of the world and back.

Charlotte.

'Come and help me make some drinks, Charlotte,' Melinda said. 'We'll leave the boys to play with the puppies.'

Charlotte smiled at her. 'Sure.'

In the kitchen, Melinda and Charlotte watched Dragan, James, Alessandro and the pups.

'Children and animals,' Melinda said quietly. 'It looks to me as if he's good with both. Bramble likes him, so I'd be happy for him to have one of the pups.'

'Thank you.'

Melinda smiled at Charlotte. 'Did you remember to bring the blanket I asked you about?'

The blanket—a thirty-centimetre square of soft fleece—was for the pup to lie on and would then go with him to his new home, so he had a familiar scent to help him settle in. Charlotte took it from her shoulder bag and handed it to Melinda. 'I haven't said anything to James, yet—I'm planning a surprise.' One that she knew he'd love; watching him play with the pups and chat to Dragan and Alessandro, as well as hearing him talk about his boyhood dreams, had shown her how much James would love a dog in his life. And from what he'd told her on the beach, she had a feeling that he'd want to stay in Cornwall now. Go for a less glitzy but much fuller life.

'So things are better now between you?' Melinda asked.

Charlotte nodded. 'We've talked. We understand each other. And Pandora even curls up on his lap.'

'That's real progress.' Melinda paused. 'I know it's been tough, but don't let the paparazzi come between you, Charlotte. Dragan and I nearly did, and we would've regretted it for the rest of our lives.'

Charlotte knew Melinda was right.

And she also knew that it was time to move her relationship with James on a step further.

Starting tonight.

CHAPTER THIRTEEN

LATER that evening, James cooked dinner back at his house—chicken breasts stuffed with Brie and wrapped in bacon, served with new potatoes and steamed green beans, followed by raspberries and rich vanilla ice cream.

'Bliss,' Charlotte said when they'd finished. 'If you ever get bored with being a surgeon...'

He grinned. 'What, you're offering me a job as your personal cook?'

She laughed. 'I'm not sure I could afford your rates.'

'We could always negotiate.' He took her hand. 'Come and sit down.'

She ended up sitting on his lap, cuddled into him, and she could feel the beat of his heart against the palm of her hand, strong and steady. Like the man himself.

She knew what she wanted.

Only...not here.

And to say it outright felt too tacky. So she picked a more oblique way. 'James, sorry to be a pain, but I'm feeling a bit...you know...Do you mind if I go home?'

He masked his disappointment quickly, though Charlotte was gratified to notice it.

'Of course. I'll drive you back.'

'And I, um, need to stop at the supermarket on the way. You know, for, um...supplies.'

She knew full well what he'd think, but she had something else entirely in mind.

'Sure,' he said.

As he drove into the supermarket car park, he asked, 'Do you want me to go in and get them for you? And have you got paracetamol and a hot-water bottle?'

Her heart warmed. Despite his flashy exterior, James was a good man at heart. A thoughtful man. And tonight was going to be…special. 'I'd rather get the stuff myself, if you don't mind. I won't be long.'

Once back at her house, James insisted on seeing her to her door—just as she knew he would.

'Would you like to come in?' she asked.

He frowned. 'I thought you were feeling a bit rough?'

'You can still come in for a few minutes. If you'd like to.'

He smiled ruefully. 'I'm selfish enough to want a bit more time with you—so, yes, please. I've really enjoyed today and I loved seeing the puppies. A coffee would be nice, if you're sure that's OK.'

She closed the door behind them. 'I'm not planning to make coffee right now.' She paused. 'But I'll make you some tomorrow morning, if you like. With *pain au chocolat.*'

He stared at her. 'Charlotte, are you saying what I think you're saying?'

'Uh-huh.'

'But I thought you…?'

'A little bit of misdirection.' She felt her face heat. 'I just wanted the first time to be here. Not on the eye-watering tones of your duvet.'

He folded his arms in mock indignation. 'There's nothing wrong with it. Those are Mediterranean colours, I'll have you know.'

'And this is Cornwall,' she pointed out.

'Which is the nearest this country's climate gets to the Mediterranean…' His teasing smile faded. 'Charlotte, I really wasn't expecting this. I don't have anything with me. I'm not prepared.'

'I am. That's why I asked you to stop at the supermarket.'

'I thought you were feeling rough because your period was due any time now.'

'I know.' She stroked his face. 'But I could hardly say to you in the car that I wanted to go to bed with you—could I?'

He actually quivered.

'Whereas, here…Come to bed with me, James.'

He swallowed hard. 'Are you sure about this?'

Oh, hell. She'd miscalculated this. Badly. He was obviously trying to let her down gently. She wrapped her arms round herself, mortified and wishing she'd kept her mouth shut. 'Sorry. I presumed.'

'No.' He shook his head frantically. 'No, no, no, no, no. It's got nothing to do with me not wanting to go to bed with you. I *do*. I just want to be sure you don't feel pressured.'

'I feel safe with you.'

He leaned over and brushed his mouth against hers. 'Charlotte, if you're sure, then I'd like nothing more than to make love with you, right now. But I also want to make it clear that if you want me to stop, all you have to do is tell me and I stop.' His gaze held hers. 'And that means at *any* point, Charlotte. Even if we're skin to skin. Even if I'm inside you.'

James. Inside her. The thought made her heart skitter.

And he'd be prepared to stop at such a point, regardless of his own discomfort?

'Thank you,' she said quietly.

'Though I'm definitely feeling the pressure,' he admitted. 'I just hope I can live up to your expectations and make it good for you.'

It was her turn to kiss him lightly. 'Sex is supposed to be fun, James.' The last time for her had been a painful ordeal. But she knew that James would change all that. He'd make some new memories with her, to wipe out the bad ones. 'So let's just enjoy this. Let's draw a line through my past—and yours. I'm not Sophia, and you're not Michael.'

He took her hand and drew it up to his mouth, making her knees go weak. 'That's true. Take me to bed, Charlotte.'

She led him upstairs to her room.

James wasn't surprised to discover that Charlotte's bedroom was as calm and restful as Charlotte herself: decorated in tones of duck-egg blue, eau-de-nil and white. Her double bed had a wrought-iron frame, painted white.

She switched on the bedside light—one that clearly had several levels of brightness, as it was bright enough for him to see her face and be aware of her responses, but not so bright as to be overpowering—and closed the curtains.

And then, slowly, she walked over towards him.

She'd been close to him before. She'd waltzed with him. Kissed him. Sat on his lap. Spent the night with him—albeit with a duvet chastely between them.

But this was different.

The ultimate closeness.

The first time she'd made love since Michael.

She'd chosen a man who'd dated some of the most beautiful women in the world. And *he* thought he was feeling the pressure?

Charlotte's fingers fumbled with the buttons on his shirt, too shaky to undo them.

Gently, he lifted her hands to his mouth. Kissed each finger in turn. 'We can stop any time you like,' he reassured her again.

'I know, and it's not that. It's…' How could she explain, without sounding ridiculous or needy? And it wasn't that she was putting herself down: she was comfortable in her own skin. She just wanted this to be perfect. Which was crazy: how could a first time be perfect? 'It's been a while for me,' she said.

'It doesn't matter. Tonight we're going to learn a bit more about each other. Discover what each other likes. It's going to be a journey of pleasure, Charlotte. And we can take as long as we like, stop when we like. No rush, no pressure. Just you and me.' He pressed a feather-light kiss against her eyelids, the tip of her nose, her cheekbones. Reassuring her. 'You know what?' he said. 'I've just had a brilliant idea.'

'What?'

'You're the captain of the quiz team. So it's a fair bet you have a trivia game.'

'Ye-es.' Where was he going with this?

'Go and get it,' he said. 'Because I'm going to challenge you.'

She felt her eyes widen in surprise. 'Challenge me?'

'Uh-huh. Except we're changing a couple of the rules, and we're not going to play on a board—just the cards will do.'

'What kind of rules?' she asked.

'If you get the question right, you can take off an item of my clothing. If I get the question right, I can take off an item of yours.'

'Strip trivia?'

'With a twist,' he confirmed, smiling.

She fetched the trivia game from the cupboard in her living room and handed it over to him.

He took a set of quiz cards from the box. 'Right. I'll go first.'

'Why?'

'Because I'm the guest, and you have to be polite to me.'

She knew exactly what he was doing—and she loved him for it.

Loved him, full stop.

He got the first question right. 'That's a shoe to me,' he said.

She allowed him to remove her left shoe, and copied his choice when she got her question right.

He opted for a shoe with his second question, as did she; but he got the third question wrong. Deliberately, she was sure. To reassure her that they'd take this at her speed.

Though she was ready for this. She knew this was the right

thing, for both of them. So when she got her third question right, she smiled at him. 'That's your shirt.'

He spread his hands. 'Take it.'

She reached out to undo the buttons of his shirt, and this time her fingers did as they were told. She tugged his shirt out of the waistband of his jeans, flattened her palms against his chest, and then burst out laughing.

'What?'

'You're always so perfectly groomed—I suppose a bit of me wondered whether you'd wax your chest,' she confessed.

He laughed. 'I'm really *not* that vain, Charlotte.'

'No?' She ruffled his perfectly groomed hair. 'That's better—James, you're so perfect that it makes you a bit…well, scary.'

'I think there was a compliment buried under that lot,' he said. 'But perfect…no, I'm just a man.' He looked at her. 'Your man,' he amended softly. 'If you want me.'

Her mouth went dry. 'I do.'

'Good. Hold that thought.' He won the next question. 'Your T-shirt, I think. May I?' At her nod, his fingers dipped beneath the hem of her T-shirt and stroked her midriff. She remembered seeing his surgeon's hands at work, deft and precise—and she really wanted to feel those hands against her body, feel them coaxing a response from her. Slowly, he bunched the soft cotton upwards, stroking her skin as he did so. 'Your skin's so soft, Charlotte. You feel beautiful. You *are* beautiful,' he said, his voice quiet and intense, as he removed her T-shirt completely. He traced the lacy outline of her bra with a fingertip. 'I like this. It's pretty.' He pushed the straps down, and nuzzled the bare skin of her shoulders. 'Mmm, you taste nice.' He breathed in her scent. 'You smell nice, too.'

'Uh, I thought this was one question, one item of clothing removed?'

'Rule change, as of now,' he said. 'You're allowed to touch the skin you uncover.'

'Strictly speaking,' she said, 'you're cheating—because you moved my bra straps and you hadn't actually won the question to do that.'

'Guilty as charged.' He spread his hands. 'So I guess that's your choice of forfeit.'

Her heart rate speeded up a notch. 'A kiss.'

He tilted her chin up towards him with his index finger and kissed her lightly; she closed her eyes as his lips traced a path along the curve of her throat, and she tipped her head back, giving him access. He found the pulse beating madly at the base of her neck and lingered there a while before tracing a slow exploratory path along the sensitive curve of her neck.

'Forfeit paid in full,' she said shakily.

He dropped a kiss on her shoulder, straightened up and smiled at her. 'Pity. I'll have to do some more cheating, I think.'

He lost his jeans in the next round, and her mouth went dry. She lost her jeans next, but she couldn't think straight enough to work on the next question.

'Your bra, I think,' he said, and unclipped it with one hand.

'That,' she said, 'was a bit smooth.'

He grinned. 'Blame it on my misspent youth.'

She could believe it. James Alexander had probably charmed every female within a ten-mile radius from the moment of his first smile.

'But there are two things you should know about me,' he said. 'Firstly, I'm never, ever unfaithful. And, secondly, whatever the gossip rags claim about me, I'm a bit fussy about who I go to bed with.'

'I'm glad to hear it. I'm fussy, too.'

He traced her lower lip with the pad of his thumb. 'So that makes two of us with high standards.' He let her bra fall to the floor and gave a sharp intake of breath. 'Charlotte, you're incredibly beautiful.' He cupped her breasts and teased her hardening nipples with the pads of his thumbs. He dipped his head and took one nipple into his mouth, teased it with his tongue and his teeth until she shivered; then he stopped. 'OK?' His voice was full of concern.

'More than OK,' she whispered, knowing that she could trust him.

'I'm not entirely sure either of us is going to get another question right,' he said.

'So what do you suggest?'

He put the cards away. 'That we cheat,' he said, and drew her gently into his arms.

She wasn't sure which of them removed the last vestiges of each other's clothing, but the next thing she knew they were naked beneath the sheets and exploring each other with hands and lips and tongues—and oh, it felt glorious to have those clever surgeon's hands stroking her skin and teasing her nipples and gently parting her thighs.

James ripped the foil packet open and slid the condom on to protect her, then lay back against her pillows, grasped the wrought-iron headboard, and gave her a smile that managed to be sweet and utterly sinful at the same time.

'I,' he said, 'am completely yours. Do whatever you want with me.'

Then it clicked.

He was giving her control. Giving her back what Michael had taken.

And she really, really loved him for it. For caring that much. For knowing the right thing to do and let them move forward.

She straddled him, and he sucked in a breath.

'Take it at your pace,' he said, his voice cracked. 'Only…can I ask, please don't take too long? Or I might just have to beg.'

His fingers tightened against the iron as she slid her hand round his shaft and positioned him so she could sink down onto him, then lowered herself slowly, slowly, slowly.

The moment that he was fully sheathed inside her, he took

one hand from the headboard, laced his fingers through hers and whispered, 'Charlotte.'

His were dark and soulful and sweet.

'What?'

He drew their linked hands to his mouth and kissed the backs of her fingers. 'Thank you. For trusting me.'

She smiled back. 'Thank you. For taking the shadows away.'

At that, he shifted so that he, too, was sitting, released her hands, and wrapped his arms round her. 'This is probably the worst timing in the world,' he said, resting his cheek against hers and holding her close, 'but there's something I need to say.'

'What's that?'

He drew back just enough so she could see the sincerity in his face. 'I love you.'

She blinked. 'Did you just say…?'

'I love you,' he repeated, and smiled wryly. 'I almost told you, that time we were walking on the beach and I explained about Sophia. But it wasn't the right time.'

'And now is?'

'Probably not,' he admitted. 'But I'll tell you again. After.'

'After what?'

He gave her a grin of sheer devilry. 'After I've made you come.'

His words alone made her heart skitter, and as she moved over him, she could feel her body racing towards the peak.

Just as her climax hit, James tightened his arms around her.

'I love you,' he said, burying his face in the curve between her shoulder and neck, and she felt his body surge against hers.

CHAPTER FOURTEEN

THE next morning, Charlotte woke up alone; but there was a dent in the pillow that told her she hadn't dreamed it—James had spent the night with his body curved protectively round hers.

The scent of fresh coffee told her that he was downstairs. Just as she was thinking it, her bedroom door opened, and he walked in, carrying two mugs. He was wearing nothing but a towel, slung low around his hips. And he looked so gorgeous that she couldn't think straight.

'Good morning,' he said with a smile.

'Morning,' she mumbled.

He placed the coffee on her bedside table, then dropped the towel and climbed in next to her. 'I hope you don't mind me hijacking your kitchen. And I've fed Pandora. I don't know if I've given her enough breakfast, but I'm sure she'll complain to you later if I haven't.'

'You'll know. She'll come and miaou in your ear,' Charlotte said with a wry smile.

'Just in case you've forgotten what I said last night—I love you, Charlotte,' he told her, settling back against the pillows and shifting her into his arms. 'I think I fell for you pretty early on, and the more I got to know you, the more I liked you. And these last few days, since we've sorted things out between us…it's made a few things clear to me. What I want out of life.'

'And what's that?' she asked.

'I could tell you—but I don't want to pressurise you. And I still don't know how you feel about me.'

She coughed. 'You're the first man I've allowed this close to me since Michael. What does that tell you?'

'I hope I know,' he said, 'but I'd rather you told me. Just in case I'm wrong.'

'That you're special.' She paused for just long enough to make him squirm, then grinned. 'I love you, too.'

He leaned over and kissed her. 'Good. Then all's right with my world.' And all was very much right with her world, too.

The next week passed in a blur; Charlotte and James were both incredibly busy at work. On Friday, Millie Fowler's parents brought their baby back in as her tetralogy episodes had become more frequent. James reviewed the echo with Charlotte, and came in with her to see the Fowlers.

'She's still too little for surgery,' James said, 'so I'm going to do what's called BT shunt. The "BT" stands for Blalock-Taussig—it's basically a tube that I'll place between her aorta and her pulmonary artery.'

Charlotte drew a swift diagram. 'That's from here to here,' she explained.

'It means she'll get enough blood flowing to her lungs and will stop her having so many tetralogy episodes between now and her operation,' James explained. 'I'll remove it then.'

'And in the meantime I'll see Millie regularly and we'll keep an eye on her,' Charlotte said. 'James and I work closely together, so he'll always know what's going on.'

'You do seem to work well as a team,' Mrs Fowler said.

James rested his hand briefly on Charlotte's shoulder and squeezed. 'We do. I'll check the theatre slots and give you a ring this afternoon to see when we can fit her in.'

'Is she…is she going to…?' Mr Fowler clearly couldn't bring himself to ask.

'She'll be fine,' Charlotte reassured him. 'James has done plenty of these operations in the past, and it'll make life a lot easier for her until she has the hole in her heart closed. It'll save you a lot of worrying, too, once the operation's over—and I'll be here with you while you're waiting for Millie to go to Theatre.' She smiled at the Fowlers. 'Everything's going to be just fine.'

On the Saturday afternoon, James discovered that there was a travelling funfair just down the road, halfway between St Piran and Penhally.

'Now, this we just have to do,' he said. 'I love fairs.'

Seeing the way his eyes sparkled, Charlotte put up no resistance. And it turned out to be enormous fun—eating candyfloss and doughnuts, spinning round on the rides. James insisted on trying every stall, and on the hoopla stall he won a plastic egg. He opened it, eyed Charlotte, and grinned.

'What's in the egg?' she asked.

'I'll show you later.' He linked his fingers through hers. 'Are you scared of heights?'

'No.'

'Good. We'll go on the big wheel next, then.'

It was late enough for the sky to be dark; the lights from the fairground glittered beneath them as they rose to the peak of the ride.

'Charlotte. There's something I need to talk to you about.'

James sounded serious, and she had to struggle to keep her own voice light. 'Sure.'

'I know I said I wouldn't rush you, but I'm really not very good at waiting for things. And I want the rest of my life to start now.'

She still wasn't with him.

And then he produced a bottle of sparkling mineral water from one pocket and the plastic egg from the other. 'Traditionally, this moment's meant to involve champagne and a diamond solitaire, but you've taught me that that stuff's just for show. The important things are what lie behind it. And the important thing is love. I love you, Charlotte. With you, the world is full of sunshine, instead of the glitzy stuff I used to have in my life as its substitute.' He opened the egg to reveal a translucent blue plastic ring decorated with three blobs in the same material. 'So will you marry me?'

He was asking her to marry him—with a plastic ring. Leaving all the glitz behind. Because he said that she'd taught him to see the important things behind the surface.

'Marry you?' she repeated, still not quite believing he'd asked her.

'The word I'm looking for is "yes",' he said softly. 'It doesn't matter whether this is water and plastic, or vintage champagne and a one-carat platinum-set diamond. They're just trappings—and I want something real. I want you. And me. And a family.'

Exactly what she wanted, and had thought would never happen for her.

She threw her arms round him and kissed him. 'Yes,' she said. 'Yes, I'll marry you. Because I love you all the way back.'

He slid the ring onto her finger. 'This is temporary,' he said.

Extremely temporary, because James took Charlotte shopping the next morning to find a ring. And then he went all mysterious on her, insisting on dropping her home for the afternoon as he had 'something to do'. Which suited her fine, as she had something to do, too.

That evening, James picked her up and took her back to his place. 'Dinner, madam, is served.' Charlotte could see how much effort he'd taken. He'd lit candles everywhere, his living room was full of flowers, and he'd set a table on the balcony so they could look out at the night sky and the sea.

And over pudding—the richest, most gorgeous chocolate mousse she'd ever eaten in her life—he gave her the ring they'd chosen together that morning, a simple band of Cornish gold set with a tanzanite that he'd said was the exact colour of her eyes.

'To us,' he said, lifting a glass of champagne, 'and the rest of our lives.'

She echoed the toast, and then handed him an envelope.

'What's this?' he asked.

'Engagement present,' she said with a smile.

He opened the envelope to reveal a photograph of a black flatcoat retriever puppy with a piece of pink ribbon round his neck.

'His name, I believe, is Dylan,' Charlotte told him. 'And he'll be ready to come and live with us towards the end of October.'

James looked steadily at her. 'Us?'

'OK, so my house isn't quite as flash as your townhouse with its sea view—but, if you don't mind downgrading for a while, you could always move in with me,' she said.

'Charlotte, with you I'd be happy to live in a beach hut,' he said, his face full of sincerity. 'I would *love* to move in with you.' He stared at the photograph. 'Every birthday, every Christmas, every summer, I asked if I could have a dog.'

'I know,' she said softly. 'And I think maybe you're ready for him now.'

'Ready to settle down. To start our family.' He paused. 'What about Pandora?'

'Melinda says you can introduce a pup into a house with a cat much more easily than a kitten into a house with dogs,' Charlotte reassured him. 'Burmese blues are really sociable, and Pandora's really come out of her shell with you. She'll be fine with Dylan, too; she'll probably smack him on the nose to keep him in line, but she'll also probably cuddle up with him.'

'A dog, a cat, a future and a family.' He smiled at her. 'Charlotte, you've just made all my dreams come true.'

'It's mutual,' she said softly. 'Until you, I didn't think I'd ever find love. I'd stopped looking.'

'Me, too,' James said. 'But we've found each other. For keeps.'

EPILOGUE

Six months later: late afternoon on an April Saturday

JAMES glanced at his watch. Two minutes to go. Was Charlotte going to hold with tradition and be late? Sophia had kept everyone waiting for nearly twenty minutes...

'Relax,' Jack said. 'This isn't like the last time.' He smiled. 'For a start, you're marrying the right woman.'

'Yeah.' James smiled back at his best man. Jack was right. This was nothing like his wedding with Sophia. Instead of having all the cloak-and-dagger stuff, the ridiculous security, he and Charlotte had talked to the press and done a deal: they'd pose for photographs after the wedding in return for a decent donation to hospital funds and being left alone to enjoy the rest of their wedding.

A small wedding, with just their closest family and friends attending. Not people who wanted to boost their celebrity rating, people who were coming to the wedding because they wanted to celebrate James and Charlotte's happiness. A wedding full of love rather than bling.

Admittedly they were having the wedding in the most upmarket hotel in St Piran, and were holding the reception there, too; Charlotte had agreed to compromise that far.

James had stayed at the hotel the previous night, with his parents and his brother Mark, while Charlotte had stayed in their new house with her parents. Melinda and Dragan had been kind enough to take in Dylan and Pandora for the weekend, because Charlotte had worried in case the cat and the pup wouldn't settle into boarding kennels.

And today she was going to marry him. Pledge her love in front of the people they loved most.

He glanced at his watch again. And almost exactly at the moment the second hand reached the number twelve, Jack nudged him and the first notes of Bach's 'Jesu, Joy of Man's Desiring' floated into the air, played by a solo cellist.

She was here.

James had a huge lump in his throat as he turned to see his bride walk towards him, holding her father's arm and wearing the dress she'd managed to keep a secret from him over the last few weeks. A knee-length confection in lilac taffeta, with a sweetheart neckline, matching lilac high-heeled court shoes and lavender pearls. She was carrying a bouquet of white roses and white tulips with frilly lilac edges; her hair was loose, in a mass of soft waves, and James had never seen her look more beautiful.

'I love you,' he said as she joined him in front of the registrar.

She smiled at him, a smile that reached her eyes and made the whole room feel as if it were bathed in sunshine. 'I love you, too.'

'And I can't tell you how much I'm looking forward to the rest of our life together.'

She laughed. 'I thought about being late. But then I remembered that my husband-to-be isn't the patient type.'

'I can learn. Everything's possible, with you by my side.'

The rest of the ceremony was a blur, as were the photographs afterwards, but James felt as if his smile was a mile wide. All through the formal meal, he kept looking at his bride and kept wanting to pinch himself to make sure he wasn't dreaming— that he really had got this lucky.

And then finally it was the evening reception. A reception with a slight difference—because they'd merged two homes and had everything, Charlotte has asked people to donate tombola prizes rather than give wedding presents. All the proceeds were going to be split between the rape crisis centre and the hospital. And so far people had been incredibly generous, both with their donations and with buying tickets.

Charlotte had sold tombola tickets to all the paparazzi, too. Even the most hard-bitten snapper had softened at her smile and paid up with pleasure.

The first dance was a proper waltz, played only on the piano: Tchaikovsky's 'Sleeping Beauty' waltz. Charlotte had suggested it: 'It reminds me of the moment I fell in love with you, James. The night you gave me a dress that made me feel like a princess and danced with me—and kissed me.'

It was a precious memory for him, too. And he knew he'd remember this moment for the rest of his life. Holding his bride in his arms, dancing with her in perfect teamwork.

As the last notes died away, James spirited Charlotte out to the balcony. The stars were just coming out and they could see the moon reflected on the sea.

'I hope you didn't mind us having glitzy ballroom dancing for the reception,' he said, stroking her face.

'Given your penchant for flashy things,' she teased, 'I could hardly object.'

'Hey, sometimes you need to put on a bit of glitz.' He kissed her, feeling her mouth open beneath his and feeling as if he'd finally come home. 'But the important thing is what's behind the glitz,' he said softly. 'With you, I know I've got the most important things in life—things that a year ago I never thought I'd know. Trust, and love.'

'Me, too,' Charlotte said softly. 'You've taught me to trust again.' And then she laughed.

'What?'

'Listen,' she said.

He did. The band was playing 'True Love', from the film *high society*.

'This,' she said, 'could be our song. Admittedly you're the one with the posh background, and I'm just an ord—'

He spun her round and kissed the rest of the words from her lips. 'There's nothing remotely ordinary about you, Charlotte Alexander. But the sentiment behind the song's about right. I love you. For ever. And I'll always be true.'

She kissed him back. 'I love you, too, James. Truly. And for ever.'

MILLS & BOON

OCTOBER 2009 HARDBACK TITLES

ROMANCE

The Billionaire's Bride of Innocence	Miranda Lee
Dante: Claiming His Secret Love-Child	Sandra Marton
The Sheikh's Impatient Virgin	Kim Lawrence
His Forbidden Passion	Anne Mather
The Mistress of His Manor	Catherine George
Ruthless Greek Boss, Secretary Mistress	Abby Green
Cavelli's Lost Heir	Lynn Raye Harris
The Blackmail Baby	Natalie Rivers
Da Silva's Mistress	Tina Duncan
The Twelve-Month Marriage Deal	Margaret Mayo
And the Bride Wore Red	Lucy Gordon
Her Desert Dream	Liz Fielding
Their Christmas Family Miracle	Caroline Anderson
Snowbound Bride-to-Be	Cara Colter
Her Mediterranean Makeover	Claire Baxter
Confidential: Expecting!	Jackie Braun
Snowbound: Miracle Marriage	Sarah Morgan
Christmas Eve: Doorstep Delivery	Sarah Morgan

HISTORICAL

Compromised Miss	Anne O'Brien
The Wayward Governess	Joanna Fulford
Runaway Lady, Conquering Lord	Carol Townend

MEDICAL™

Hot-Shot Doc, Christmas Bride	Joanna Neil
Christmas at Rivercut Manor	Gill Sanderson
Falling for the Playboy Millionaire	Kate Hardy
The Surgeon's New-Year Wedding Wish	Laura Iding

0909 Gen Std LP

OCTOBER 2009 LARGE PRINT TITLES

ROMANCE

The Billionaire's Bride of Convenience	Miranda Lee
Valentino's Love-Child	Lucy Monroe
Ruthless Awakening	Sara Craven
The Italian Count's Defiant Bride	Catherine George
Outback Heiress, Surprise Proposal	Margaret Way
Honeymoon with the Boss	Jessica Hart
His Princess in the Making	Melissa James
Dream Date with the Millionaire	Melissa McClone

HISTORICAL

His Reluctant Mistress	Joanna Maitland
The Earl's Forbidden Ward	Bronwyn Scott
The Rake's Inherited Courtesan	Ann Lethbridge

MEDICAL™

A Family For His Tiny Twins	Josie Metcalfe
One Night With Her Boss	Alison Roberts
Top-Notch Doc, Outback Bride	Melanie Milburne
A Baby for the Village Doctor	Abigail Gordon
The Midwife and the Single Dad	Gill Sanderson
The Playboy Firefighter's Proposal	Emily Forbes

NOVEMBER 2009 HARDBACK TITLES

ROMANCE

Ruthless Magnate, Convenient Wife	Lynne Graham
The Prince's Chambermaid	Sharon Kendrick
The Virgin and His Majesty	Robyn Donald
Innocent Secretary...Accidentally Pregnant	Carol Marinelli
Bought: The Greek's Baby	Jennie Lucas
Powerful Italian, Penniless Housekeeper	India Grey
Count Toussaint's Pregnant Mistress	Kate Hewitt
Forgotten Mistress, Secret Love-Child	Annie West
The Boselli Bride	Susanne James
In the Tycoon's Debt	Emily McKay
The Girl from Honeysuckle Farm	Jessica Steele
One Dance with the Cowboy	Donna Alward
The Daredevil Tycoon	Barbara McMahon
Hired: Sassy Assistant	Nina Harrington
Just Married!	Cara Colter & Shirley Jump
The Italian's Forgotten Baby	Raye Morgan
The Doctor's Rebel Knight	Melanie Milburne
Greek Doctor Claims His Bride	Margaret Barker

HISTORICAL

Tall, Dark and Disreputable	Deb Marlowe
The Mistress of Hanover Square	Anne Herries
The Accidental Countess	Michelle Willingham

MEDICAL™

Posh Doc, Society Wedding	Joanna Neil
Their Baby Surprise	Jennifer Taylor
A Mother for the Italian's Twins	Margaret McDonagh
New Boss, New-Year Bride	Lucy Clark

1009 Gen Std LP

MILLS & BOON

NOVEMBER 2009 LARGE PRINT TITLES

ROMANCE

The Greek Tycoon's Blackmailed Mistress	Lynne Graham
Ruthless Billionaire, Forbidden Baby	Emma Darcy
Constantine's Defiant Mistress	Sharon Kendrick
The Sheikh's Love-Child	Kate Hewitt
The Brooding Frenchman's Proposal	Rebecca Winters
His L.A. Cinderella	Trish Wylie
Dating the Rebel Tycoon	Ally Blake
Her Baby Wish	Patricia Thayer

HISTORICAL

The Notorious Mr Hurst	Louise Allen
Runaway Lady	Claire Thornton
The Wicked Lord Rasenby	Marguerite Kaye

MEDICAL™

The Surgeon She's Been Waiting For	Joanna Neil
The Baby Doctor's Bride	Jessica Matthews
The Midwife's New-found Family	Fiona McArthur
The Emergency Doctor Claims His Wife	Margaret McDonagh
The Surgeon's Special Delivery	Fiona Lowe
A Mother For His Twins	Lucy Clark